THE DEMI-TASSE DÉBUT

A LORA WEAVER MYSTERY PREQUEL NOVELLA

KATY LEEN

ISBN: print: 978-1-9990767-1-9

Cover: Team KL

Cover illustration by Adrienne Alexander

Cover background icons: The Noun Project, book #8161971

*For readers
of the Lora Weaver series everywhere.
This one's for you :)*

1

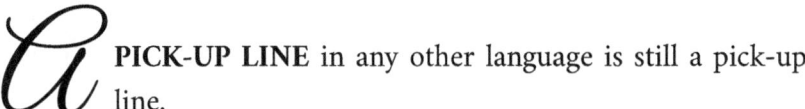**PICK-UP LINE** in any other language is still a pick-up line.

Even if I didn't understand a word of it.

I looked up at the man speaking to me in French. He was tall with shoulders broad enough to suggest he worked out but not so broad to suggest he mixed steroids into his orange juice at breakfast. He was dressed in a T-shirt and jeans and wore scuffed sandals that looked like they'd just come from a day at the beach.

With a demure shake of my head, I offered him a low *non merci,* but he remained standing to the side of the teensy table where I sat in the teensy café that had beckoned me in with its vintage mismatched chairs and vibrant mismatched coffee cups. And maybe most importantly of all, its whirring air-conditioning. After the morning I'd had, I was in desperate need of a reprieve from the sauna outdoors trying to pass itself off as just another summer's day.

If I'd known summers in Montréal could be just as smoldering as back in New York, I never would have moved here. Okay, maybe that's not true. I agreed faster than it took me to blink when my boyfriend, Adam, had asked me to accompany him to his hometown. And when it wasn't playing mix'n'match with blistering heat and sweltering humidity, I loved the city. From its cobblestone walkways to its vast parklands to its array of one-way-streets. I loved the museums and the endless summer street festivals and the French air of *je ne sais quoi* that made strolling in the park seem far more essential than running the rat race.

I heard the rustle of chair feet on tile floor and pick-up-line man sat down across from me, pulled out a journal, and began jotting notes in the pages. Not looking at me even once.

The tingly warmth on my skin, faded thanks to the air-conditioning, started to flame again. Maybe I had it wrong. Maybe the guy just wanted a place to sit. Perfect strangers shared tables all the time in popular restaurants during busy times. And one perusal of the place told me it was definitely busy time. Nary an empty seat in sight. Maybe I had misunderstood the pick-up line after all. Since arriving in Montréal, I'd brushed away over a dozen years of dust from my high-school French and trotted it out gleefully only to realize my teacher had been generous with my C grade for the class. Maybe what the guy had asked was more like "Is this seat taken?" and the shake of my head gave him the go-ahead to join me.

I rearranged my *mochaccino glacé* and croissant in front of me, fidgeting to hide my embarrassment. Jumping to conclusions was not a sport I played often. Or well, apparently.

I went back to the novel I'd brought with me to read on the métro. The carnation, bought earlier from a street vendor for luck and tucked into the book's pages, still marked the same place it had then, my mind too tense to read on the way downtown and too dejected after I'd left my appointment. A job interview. The latest in a string of interviews that went exactly the same. My education, impeccable. My nearly ten years experience as a social worker in New York, impressive. My lack of French skills, impassable. As in a deal-breaker. A roadblock, as it were, to my getting any position in a city that requires bilingualism for jobs in my field. Or possibly, stellar unilingual skills, so long as that uni language is French.

"It's not personal," one interviewer had said. "It's just the law here for organizations like us. We can't hire candidates without at least some good French." A sympathetic smile capped her words.

I'd smiled back, clutching the sheet of references I'd brought that would once again go unused, wanting to ask if she might be so kind as to list any organizations that may hire candidates like me. But I knew better than to bother. Having already sat through identical conversations at other interviews, I feared the answer would be a confused look and a head shake. If there were any social work jobs in Montréal that accepted English-only workers like me I was sure the jobs would be few and far between, in high demand, and likely once secured, kept until retirement.

I perched my book at the edge of the café table, beside my croissant plate, and made myself read a paragraph. Either I could sit here and brood about my unemployment or I could escape into the British countryside and manor house life of the nineteenth century, and I was choosing escape.

Every few words my eyes drifted upwards, to my table mate's notebook, the zip of his pen crossing the small pages in swift streaks, his movement causing our table to rock onto its one short leg and back again. The man's head bent forward and his hair, wound at the crown like dark rotini, dipped so close to me I caught a hint of musky scent from his shampoo.

I peered at his scrawl, a skeletal printing tough to make out upside down. Not English I thought. But same alphabet. Likely French, or Italian maybe, definitely some kind of accents over letters.

At the end of a page, he paused and checked a text on his phone then flipped the book closed, drank down his espresso in one shot like it was booze, and looked straight at me.

I smiled, hoping he hadn't noticed my brief perusal of his notes. My chair jostled, once and then again, and I let my eyes travel from the man to the ground where a white rubber wheel ensnared my chair leg. The wheel belonged to a stroller. The stroller to a young mom with a toddler snoozing, chin to chest in the seat, and another child, a girl maybe five years old, sweaty, one elbow held aloft smeared with dirt and fresh blood. The girl dragged a scooter and wore a bright pink helmet tilted sideways on her head, straps dangling open at her neck. Tendrils escaped the mom's tangerine braid of hair, her skin glistened, and her eyes had the look of someone in desperate need of caffeine. And a place to rest her weary feet.

I stood to untangle the wheel from my chair and whisked my book back into my bag. "Here," I said. "Take my seat. I'm just finishing up."

The mom glanced at my nearly-full *mochaccino glacé* and my uneaten croissant.

"No really," I said. "I, um, was going to move to the patio to get some sun." Okay, this was a lie, but lies didn't count when they were white ones for good causes.

The girl limped to my chair and sat, taking me at my word. While she hopped up, I held the wood back of the chair firmly, noticing that my pick-up-line friend had vacated his side of the table and was nowhere to be seen. Quickly I gathered up his leftover espresso cup and my own things and smiled at the mom who gratefully sank into the man's vacant chair and thanked me, her accent French but her words perfect English.

I thought of offering to watch the toddler while the mom took the girl to the bathroom to wash off her bloody elbow but knew that babysitting may not be a welcome suggestion from a stranger, so I offered to get her some wet napkins instead. She declined, thanking me again, and withdrew a package of moist wipes from the diaper bag draped over the stroller handlebars. She passed the wipes to her daughter who cleaned up her own boo-boo, topping it with the animal print bandage her mother doled out automatically in follow-up. In the preparedness department, Boy Scouts had nothing on mothers. Mothers with diaper bags were like turtles with shells. Wherever they went, they carried all the comforts of home. Or at least the important ones.

The mom dropped the daughter's used wipe into a tiny bag draped from the side of the stroller near a cup holder. She pulled a coloring book and set of crayons from the mess of toys and books brightly covered in flowers, trucks, and kittens crammed into a basket below the snoozing child, and she passed the crayons to the little girl who waved me off with a shy smile.

To make good on my lie, I went out to the patio, more courtyard than terrace, surprised to find it, too, quite crowded. Flagstones on the ground, the area was longer than it was wide, the width as narrow as the café interior, the length longer, extending outward buffered by a brick wall at the end, the rest lined by a short iron fence, intertwining vines covering the iron in lush green. On the outer side of the fence hung flower boxes with bright pink and white flowers. Courtyard side, marble-topped bistro tables clustered with narrow chairs made the most of every square inch, most already taken, but I managed to snag a table close to the café door, hoping to catch wafts of air-conditioning streaming out as people came and went.

Two bites into my croissant, a shadow darkened my table. Another man, glare of sun behind him catching me in the eye when I looked up.

I waited a beat for him to speak, not wanting to jump to

conclusions again, hoping this newcomer and I spoke the same language. This time, whatever the guy wanted had to be more than a seat because there were empty tables to be had.

To lessen the glare in my eyes and see the guy better, I reached down to where I'd left my purse on the ground beside me, fishing for the sunglasses I'd hooked onto the straps. The shadow above me loomed closer, swooped down, and in a flash my bag was gone. Nothing left but my department store shades dangling from my fingertips.

2

I STOOD AND stared in disbelief as the guy dashed off the flagstone patio to the cobblestone street beyond. "Hey! That's my purse," I called after him, like he didn't already know.

A woman with short blonde hair sprang up from a nearby table, leapt over the iron fence like a horse jumping pickets, and charged after the man. I made my way around the fence and followed at a jog as best I could in a short dress and sandals. The two of them zig-zagged through passersby, and I caught a glimpse of something tossed in the air. My bag!

I picked up speed, flushing from the heat. My whole life was in that bag. My wallet, my keys, my old MetroCard from New York, my best lipstick, okay my only lipstick, my mobile phone with all my contacts, the new chew toy I'd bought my dog. Maybe even my passport which I knew I should have taken out but probably hadn't. Everything.

The blonde woman caught my bag mid-air in one hand, midstride, her head forward, fixed on the distance ahead where I made out the man jumping into a car. The blonde kept her attention on the car for a moment then turned back, nearly bumping into me as I caught up with her.

She held the purse out to me and said something. More French, fast and clipped, her words stringing together like she spoke in sentence blocks rather than individual words.

"Thank you so much, er *merci*," I said.

She shrugged as though it was nothing. Like every day she rescued purses from thieves. "*Alors*. You should check it, no?"

"Excuse me?"

Her eyes darted to my purse, one of her eyebrows accentuating its curve.

"Oh right, of course." I fumbled through the contents in my bag, pulling out my wallet and passport case and inspecting them more closely. All good. Even my bank card and my credit card safely nestled in their slits.

I let out a sigh. "Thank goodness he didn't get anything," I said. "And thank goodness for you." Also thank goodness she'd switched to English. Probably when she'd heard my pitiful pronunciation of *merci*. "Please, let me at least get you another drink at the café."

She nodded and we fell into step together retracing the path back.

The food we'd each abandoned still sat on our respective tables and she gathered hers up and moved to my table. The whipped cream topping of my *mochaccino glacé* had lost its fluffy peaks, dissolving into mocha swirls on the surface, the cup warm to the touch thanks to the sun. My croissant appeared unchanged, its strawberry side-kick somewhat darker, the heat bringing out its sweet scent. The blonde's plate held remnants of something flaky, buttery sheen below, melted chocolate dotting the edges. Her tiny cup, nearly empty espresso.

I decided we could both do with a refresh and popped inside to fetch it after confirming her order.

"I'm Lora, by the way," I said when I returned with a tray of food.

"Camille." Her eyes surveyed the tray as she introduced herself and collected the espresso she'd agreed to let me get her by way of a thank you.

I noted how she pronounced her name, filing it away in my memory bank. Just two syllables. "Ka" like the beginning of cat and "Me" like me. I did not want to be one of those foreigners who botched French names. I may not be able to speak the language fluently, but I could get names right.

"*Et bien.* You must really like ice cream," Camille said.

I glanced at the two chocolate sundaes I'd bought, each topped with a cherry, no nuts. I didn't want to chance the nuts. So many people are allergic these days. Same was true of dairy but given the butter glaze on her earlier plate, I thought that much might be a safe bet.

I laughed and slipped one of the sundaes to Camille's side of the table. "This one's for you. I know you said you only wanted coffee but ice cream's good with coffee." To my way of thinking, ice cream made pretty much anything better. Plus, I thought after her mad dash in this heat, it might be cooling. Although unlike me, she hadn't seemed to even break a sweat. Surprising since along with her cotton sleeveless blouse and jean shorts, she wore ankle boots. I'd be sweltering in boots.

She shifted the mini backpack strapped to her shoulder and picked up her spoon. "*C'est génial. Merci.*"

I smiled and started in on my own sundae before it melted into a milky pool like the whipped cream in my coffee, which I revived with a fleet of ice cubes I'd scored when I was in getting the sundaes. Normally I wasn't a big coffee drinker, but I'd promised myself I'd try new things in my new city and coffee from a French café fit the bill. Plus, I hoped it would perk me up after my interview. I had not expected it would also have to get me through a purse snatching.

Camille flicked a finger at the tray. Practically empty now, the bottom revealed a replica of the Québec flag—blue and white with four *fleur-de-lys*. "I don't think those trays are for outside," she said.

"This one I bought," I confessed, flushing a tad. "There were a few mixed in with a bunch of travel mugs and coasters. I think they're for tourists, but I figure I kinda qualify since I'm from New York and new to the city."

Her face turned serious. "In that case, I apologize for my city. It's not the best welcome after all to have your purse stolen."

I tried to shrug it off but truth be told I was a bit shaken. Having Camille as a distraction was helping, though. That and my years growing up in New York and my social work training for stress management. I was starting to think courses in conflict resolution and stress management should be part of every high school curriculum. Certainly they were just as helpful life skills as any home ec class. Or algebra for that matter.

"Oh it's fine, really. Thanks to you. If you hadn't helped and gotten my purse back, I'd probably be sitting in some police station somewhere instead of here, with nothing but my book to keep me company while I waited hours to make a report."

Hmm. My book.

I rummaged in my bag, kept snugly on my lap this time around, and frowned.

"Something wrong?" Camille asked.

'It's my Jane Austen," I said. "It's not in my bag."

She raised an eyebrow at me.

"My copy of *Persuasion*, the book I was reading. It's gone."

I blinked back the early sting of tears. My parents had given me that book for my thirteenth birthday. Since then they'd both passed away and I had few mementos of them. The book, a locket of my mother's that I wore, a few boxes of odds and ends of our life together, and bits of furniture. They'd given me the book on our one and only trip to England, on my actual birthday while they treated me to an actual British tea with little sandwiches and everything. It had taken them years to save for that trip and they'd sprung the whole thing on me as a surprise. I still remembered the delicate lace and ribbon my mother had used to wrap the book, an early edition with pages like silk. And her beautiful inscription on the title page. A lot of memories were locked up in that gift. And now it was gone.

"Maybe it fell out?" Camille suggested.

I shook my head. "I don't see how. The zipper was closed when you passed the purse to me." I feigned a wipe of my mouth with my napkin, extending it to cover my cheek and sop up any signs of tears. Crying in public was the last thing I wanted. Especially in front of someone I barely knew. Usually I was good at reining in my emotions. I blamed the heat and humidity for messing with my internal control center. "But what would that guy want with my novel? If he wanted to read the book so bad, he could buy a copy at practically any bookshop. Or borrow it from the library."

"*Oui*, it's not a typical theft for sure. Did you know the man?"

"Not at all," I said, surprised at the very idea. "He just showed up at my table and grabbed my bag. I hardly even saw him." I pointed up. "The sun was in my eyes. But as he ran off, I saw he was wearing a hoodie with his head covered, which wouldn't make sense in this heat, so I'm guessing he didn't want to be seen."

Camille sipped her espresso and watched me as I spoke, focused look in her light brown eyes. I sensed another question burning behind those eyes, but she stayed quiet.

I took the opportunity to check my bag again. If I overlooked the missing book in my first perusal maybe something else was missing, too. I went through it slower this time, silently checking things off as I placed them each on the table.

A gurgled noise came from Camille's side of the table and I glanced up.

"*Je m'excuse,*" she said. "That's your *cellulaire,* that?"

She gestured at my mobile phone and I surmised *cellulaire* must mean cellular. Very similar in both English and French. If only all French words sounded so close to English I'd be fluent in no time.

I picked up my flip phone and dropped it back in my bag. "I know," I said. "It's been ages since I got a new phone, this one's nearly archaic. But it works and I hate to just throw things out for no reason." I also disliked that an increasing number of things seem to be intentionally made with limited lifespans necessitating constant upgrades, but this wasn't the time to get into that.

I glanced down the street along the path the thief had taken and scooped the rest of my stuff into my bag. Everything else accounted for just fine.

"If you don't mind," I said. "I'm going to check to see if maybe you were right and somehow the book dropped out somewhere."

I felt a bit rude being so abrupt about rushing off when we weren't even finished our food, but if there was even the slimmest possibility of finding my book, I had to take it.

"*Bien sûr.*" Camille swilled the remainder of her espresso and stood. "Let's go."

I'd expected a solo expedition, not a duo, but was grateful for the extra set of eyes. That was the thing about life, for every rat fink like the purse snatcher, there was another person just full of kind deeds like Camille to balance the scales.

3

E'D BEEN UP and down the street and no sign of my book. Camille thought maybe she'd found it by a park bench overlooking a tiny garden but no luck. I knew the minute she pointed it out. Her find was red with a glossy image on the front and my book was pale blue, no cover jacket.

"I feel awful, taking up your time like this," I told her. "You must have a million better things to do than help a stranger look for a book on the street."

Camille shrugged. The same way she had about bolting out to save my purse. Like it was no big deal. Like she didn't have somewhere better to be, something better to do. Then again, this was summer in Montréal. Maybe she didn't have any pressing commitments. People around here didn't seem to schedule their lives down to the littlest second like so many folks I'd known in New York. Not that New Yorkers didn't relax and party or go for a jog in the park. They absolutely did. But somehow it felt more planned out, time accounted for for the most part. At least for my crowd. Montrealers, on the other hand, often gave off the impression their lives weren't ruled by a clock. Or maybe that was just a summer thing. Maybe they soaked up every possible drop of outdoor leisure knowing they'd be spending most of the winter in hibernation. I'd first arrived in the city mid-winter and cold didn't begin to describe it. Jack Frost himself too frozen to nip at anyone's nose.

"It seems important to you, this book," Camille said.

"It is." I explained to her how it was a gift from my parents who'd since passed away. About the trip when they'd given it to me.

Camille had donned dark sunglasses when we'd started our search and I couldn't make out her eyes, but something in her stance appeared to shift. Almost imperceptibly. Sympathy I supposed when she'd learned about the passing of my parents.

She sat on the bench and I joined her, sitting forward some so my feet could reach the ground and match hers. With her long legs, she could lean easily on the bench back, the slight curve in the wood slats providing her lumbar support. She had to be at least half a foot taller than me, putting her at about five foot seven or eight, her body in even proportions and judging by her earlier sprint, quite fit. My own body felt more compact by comparison, similar in bone structure but more petite, and not as fit although I could pass for it on days I didn't eat too much ice cream. Her hair, short and blonde, gave her added height, too. My hair was a mass of amber waves, its volume currently restrained in a side pony-tail creating a slight buffer between us.

"What's it about?" Camille asked.

"Excuse me?"

"Your book. What's the story about?"

"You mean *Persuasion*? Oh, it's about a woman who falls madly in love and gets engaged, but is persuaded to break it off and regrets it. Then years later she gets a second chance with the ex-fiancé."

"And it works out?"

I nodded. "But if you haven't read it, I won't spoil it for you by telling more. It's really a lovely story. Maybe not one of Jane Austen's most popular but still good. Have you read any of her novels?"

Camille shook her head. "I saw a couple of the movies but never read the books."

Hmm. I'm not sure I'd ever met anybody before who hadn't read any Jane Austen. Maybe she wasn't as big in French circles. Or maybe it was a language thing. Maybe the books lost some of the magic of Austen's language in translation. I often found that was true of translations, no matter how faithful they tried to be. Authors were so particular choosing their words, the lyrical feel of their sentences. It could be impossible to capture that in foreign language renderings. Of course, maybe Camille just wasn't a big reader and was more a movie person. If this day was teaching me anything it was to be careful of making assumptions.

I scratched the bridge of my nose, prickly and in the throes, I was sure, of developing a nasty burn. That was another thing this day was teaching me. Unless I wanted my face to turn into a raisin, I'd have to start wearing sunhats. The kind with big brims. Especially if I wandered down here to the Vieux Montréal port. The sun felt more intense by the waterfront, its gleaming rays bouncing off ancient tin roofs, catching in the ornate architecture of grand churches and domes, sparkling atop rippling water of the *Fleuve Saint-Laurent*. Dotting my cheeks with freckles.

I held my hand above my eyes like a makeshift visor and stood. "Well, thanks again for all your help. I don't want to keep you anymore and really I should get going. I've got to get home and walk my dog."

I dug in my bag for my OPUS card—my pass for the Montréal bus and métro system.

"Would you like a ride? My car is not far," Camille said, her gaze shifting from my card to my face.

"Oh, no thank you. I couldn't. You've done so much already."

"*Ça me fait plaisir,*" she said and rose from the bench. "*Pis,* I owe you for the ice cream, no? That was extra. I give you a lift and then we're even, okay?"

I laughed. She was totally stretching it. She had no idea where I even lived. Montréal was a big city. And even bigger if the off-island communities were included. If I lived in one of those, she could be in the car for hours going back and forth. Fortunately, I didn't. I lived on the west side and at this time of day it wouldn't be too long a ride but still not a hop and skip away.

"You sure?" I asked her. "I'm out in NDG." NDG being the short name for Notre-Dame-de-Grâce, a middle-class, family-oriented part of town with more multi-family homes than singles, loads of trees, and cute little shops along the main streets that got lots of foot-traffic.

She waved a hand in the air dismissively. "Of course. I have you home in fifteen minutes."

I laughed again. Fifteen minutes was wishful thinking. I'd driven it with my boyfriend before and even on Sundays with low traffic, it took practically fifteen minutes just to get to our parked car and wind the way out from the cobblestone streets. Either my new acquaintance was prone to stretching all her statements or she drove a flying car straight out of *The Jetsons* TV show.

4

OKAY, SO CAMILLE'S car actually did fly. Not in the "up-in-the-sky" way maybe, but I was pretty sure its velocity bordered on airplane runway speed just prior to takeoff. Our arrival at my house more crash landing than parallel parking. As I reached for the latch to open Camille's Jetta door, I held my purse in front of me in case the airbags deployed before I got out to side-walk safety.

"*C'est jolie,*" Camille said, joining me on the sidewalk and looking towards my front porch.

The house I shared with my boyfriend was a narrow, brick, two-storey Edwardian with large guillotine windows framed by large white wood shutters. A wide white porch ran the width of the place, flower pots filled with impatience hanging from rafters at the end. To the right side of the house was a similar one slightly more boxy with rose bushes hedging the front yard, and on the left side was a driveway. Clinging to the upper house brick on the driveway side were thin, leafy green vines meandering casually across the corner as though out for a stroll.

"Thanks," I said in response to Camille's compliment about the house being *"jolie"* aka pretty, a French word even I knew. "It's not really my place. It's my boyfriend Adam's. He grew up here and just inherited it from his mom. I've only been here for a few months."

I pulled the keys from my purse and started up the steps to the front door, Camille a stair behind me. She had asked to use the washroom before she got back on the road, and considering all she'd done for me I was happy to accommodate the request.

We slipped off our shoes in the vestibule and were greeted by my dog Pong when we made it through the second door. Pong was a dachshund mutt, slightly taller than a true dachshund, her back reaching above knee level to me, her coloring a mix of caramel, cream, and black. She sniffed at Camille, the sniff turning to a tail wag after I made introductions and Camille gave the dog's ribcage a stroking pat.

"The bathroom's up at the top of the stairs," I said, easing the vestibule door closed behind us all. "You can't miss it."

Camille went up and I made my way to the kitchen at the rear of the house, passing through to the sunroom beyond to let Pong out into the backyard for her own visit to the facilities.

I tossed her a doggy snack on her return and went to wash up at the kitchen sink. The room had the rectangle shape of a small farm kitchen, the kind that had seen lots of home cooking. Original wood cabinets still in pristine shape. Windows above Formica countertop lined the back wall, the window glass clean but vintage squiggly as I looked through to the big maple tree in the yard while I rinsed my hands. Pipes creaked overhead and Camille ventured into the room as I dried my hands on a towel hanging to the side of a cabinet.

"Can I get you anything before you go?" I asked her. I shuffled over to the fridge and checked stock. "Some juice? Lemonade? A

Perrier?" I caught her eyes shift to a cake stand on the counter. "Some cake maybe?"

She nodded. I smiled, not surprised. The cake was a work of chocolate art. Freshly arrived at nearly the crack of dawn. The latest offering from doting friends and neighbors still dropping food by for Adam in the wake of his mother's recent passing. It had been nearly two months and the food train had mostly stopped, but occasionally some small item arrived. In the early days food arrived quite regularly, like meals-on-wheels deliveries, the door-bell chime going off like an oven timer at mealtime. Most of it takeout offerings brought by relatives in town for the funeral before they headed back to their lives. Some from neighbors or friends of his mom, the same group who still stopped by now and then, the cake fairy of this particular chocolate creation falling into the latter category. And she'd baked the cake herself, complete with fudgy filling and glaze and a raspberry sauce meant to be drizzled over each slice.

I cut us each a sliver, pulling the sauce pitcher from the fridge and dribbling some to the side on each plate, the cool raspberry heightening the chocolate cakey scents.

I returned the raspberry sauce to the fridge, nudging it in beside a tall cardboard carton that got me thinking maybe I should offer Camille some real food first. A proper lunch to cut our morning of sugary treats.

"How about a little Chinese food before cake?" I offered, with-drawing the carton and holding it up as exhibit A. "I've got some extra takeout here from yesterday. I could heat it up in a jiff. I've got egg rolls, vegetable fried rice, and some chow mein I think."

Camille nodded and I slid the cake dishes into the fridge for safekeeping, made us up each a plate of the Chinese food and heated her serving and then mine in the microwave. I carried the plates into the adjoining dining room, the round pine table in the kitchen occupied, brimming with boxes of papers Adam was in the midst of sorting through as part of getting his mother's estate in order.

"*Ton homme* is at work?" Camille asked.

"Excuse me?"

We were seated across from each other at my dining room table, which ran lengthwise so that I faced the window overlooking the driveway and Camille faced the kitchen. The living room to the front of the house was in view through the archway for both of us and Camille had her gaze fixed that-a-way as she spoke again. "Your boyfriend is not home?"

"He comes and goes," I said. "He designs educational computer games, so he works here a lot but sometimes he's out with the team or at client meetings and such."

I hoped she didn't ask more. I was not a techie sort and got lost when Adam explained to me all the ins and outs of his job. All I really knew was at the end of a project he had a computer game for kids to show for his time. It was how we met back in New York. I was working with a group of kids in an after-school program and he used my kids like a focus group to test one of his games, part of his work for his Master's degree. Almost eighteen months ago, back when I was gainfully employed and living in Soho. And when my *Persuasion* book was safely tucked up in my apartment.

Camille nodded. "*Pis toi*? Do you also work with computers?"

"Not me," I said. "I'm better with people. I'm a social worker." The forkful of food I held drooped a little. "Well, usually. I mean when I'm working, that is. I don't have a job here yet." I smiled like I was totally okay with that. "What about you?"

She didn't answer straight away, and I wondered if maybe she was still studying. She looked to be about my age, late twenties, thirtyish. She could be working on a doctorate or something. Or maybe she was a teacher and had the summers off, and that's why she'd been so free with her time and helped me. Given her fitness, maybe she was a phys ed teacher. Or maybe even an athlete. Definitely not the corporate type. She didn't strike me as someone with a desk job.

Camille finished the last of her food, slid her plate aside, and leaned back in her chair. "I am a *détective priveé*."

I blinked, surprised. "That's a private detective, right?" That was kinda cool. I'd never met a real PI before. Totally made sense now that she'd reacted so quickly to my purse snatching. PIs on TV were always running through the streets chasing after someone.

She nodded. "I do investigations. I help the police with crimes, lawyers with cases, people to verify their mates. Things like that."

"Wow. That's great. Like a real life version of Kinsey Millhone from the Sue Grafton novels." I smiled. "Maybe I should hire you to find my book."

One of Camille's eyebrows tipped up slightly but she said nothing. Probably wondering if I was serious.

"I know. Silly, right?" I said. In a city of two million people, four million if you included the off-island folks zipping in and out, the odds of finding whose hands my book may have landed in were less than fair. Worse than looking for a needle in a haystack. Impossible. I sighed. "I just can't believe it's gone. It was stupid. I should never have taken something so precious out of the house." It was just I'd been so nervous. I thought having the book would bring me courage for the day. And comfort. Ironic since losing it robbed me of both.

I felt tears threatening again and I stood to clear away the plates and get the cake. Pong rose from her vigil under the dining room table and followed me to the kitchen. She watched me rinse the plates and slip them in the dishwasher, and she gave me a mournful look.

"You already had your midday snack," I told her.

Her gaze swung to her bowl and returned to me.

"*Pardon?*"

I startled at the female voice. Camille calling from the dining room. But with her out of my sight, for a second it was like Pong spoke, and with a French accent no less. Like even she was mastering the language before I had.

"Sorry," I called back to Camille. "I was talking to the dog. I'll just grab the cake." My eyes flitted to the kettle on the stovetop. "What about if I add some tea to that? I could whip up a batch of iced tea in no time."

"Sure," Camille said, appearing in the doorway between the kitchen and the dining room, mobile phone in her hand. Her phone gleamed in its sleek, slim glory, putting my own clunker phone to shame. If mobiles had celebrity magazines, I was sure mine would appear on one of those pages of Worst Dressed with a giant red arrow calling out its flip seam like a panty line.

Camille's phone lit up briefly, she scanned the screen, and tucked it in her short's pocket as it went black.

Okay, probably now she did have somewhere else to be and I was infringing on her time. And probably she was too polite to say anything. What was I thinking? Was I really going to hire her to find my book? That was crazy. I didn't even have a job. How would I pay her? Barter with tea and cake? It wasn't even my cake.

I shoved the kettle under the tap at the kitchen sink and flicked on the water. It wasn't like I could disinvite her, though, or keep asking if she had other plans and would prefer to be on her way. My mother had taught me better manners than that.

Pong barked, and I turned to see her scurry to the hall and make her way to the vestibule door, nose to the ground, sniffing the tiny gap of space between the door and the floor. She stepped aside when the door opened and my boyfriend Adam strode in. Adam's cropped brown hair, the color of tree bark, met his forehead in a line of sweat, and his lanky body was dressed in casual work attire, messenger bag housing his laptop swung over his shoulder. He let his bag slide from his arm to the floor, dropped his keys in a little dish on a side table, gave Pong a pat, and continued on towards the kitchen.

"Hmm. Tea," he said, eyes darting to the kettle in my hand. "In this heat? Is that for comfort or congratulations? I know you come from a line of Brits, but I don't know all the tea customs. Does that mean you got the job?"

"It's gonna be iced tea. And it means we have company," I told him, my tone bright and upbeat. I did not want to talk about jobs. I didn't want to tell him I lost out on another one. I especially didn't want to get into it in front of a virtual stranger. Even if she was the good Samaritan kind of stranger. She didn't need to know about my ever-growing list of failed interviews.

Adam's head pivoted to where Camille now sat at the kitchen table strewn with paperwork. His eyes darted to me and I made introductions. He crossed over to shake Camille's hand in greeting, and a pink rose dropped at her feet.

Camille and I both looked at the flower, two of its petals had dropped off and Adam scrambled to pick the lot up before Pong got to it.

Several more roses materialized from behind his back and he stretched out the bunch to me, his face reddening some. "Here," he said. "These were meant for you. You know, in case, the interview went well." His voice added a questioning at the end and a small smile came to his mouth. "Or, as a cheer up in case it didn't."

"Thanks," I said, accepting the flowers from him, careful to avoid touching any thorns. Not easy considering the mismatched lengths of the stems. I suspected the neighbors' rose bushes next door may be down a few buds.

I set the kettle on the stove, started the heat, and searched the cupboards for a vase. Slowly and gently opening doors and scanning the shelves. I'd been living in the house for months and I was making peace with using dishware and cookery, but poking through Adam's mother's more personal items still made me feel like an intruder. Any flowers that had come in the wake of her death had come in their own containers or Adam had dealt with them. This was my first time having my own need for a vase. I finally spied one on the top shelf in the walk-in-pantry.

"Here," Adam said, coming up behind me and shuffling me out of the way. "Let me get that."

I slid aside easily. Top shelves were not my thing. With his height of six feet and added length of an outstretched arm, top shelves were easy reach for him.

"Who is she?" Adam whispered to me, taking advantage of our sojourn in the pantry.

The "she" in question, I figured to be Camille. "I met her today," I told him. "I'll tell you more later."

"You just met her and brought her to the house? A complete stranger?" Adam's eyes were wide and his chin stiffened. We faced each other now, squished together, snap of his pants pressing into me, waft of his sweat escaping the open collar of his short-sleeve shirt, enlarged blue checks on his shirt meeting my eyes.

"It's fine," I said. "She's fine. Very nice."

The tea kettle sang and I shimmied away and out to the kitchen. Adam so close behind I heard him grunt not two steps into the room. I paused to see the cause and saw he was looking at Camille, crouched over the kitchen table, cell phone in hand, and looming above papers belonging to Adam's mother.

5

"**S**HUSH," **I SAID** to Adam. "She's barely out the front door. And she didn't take pictures of your mother's files."

"You don't know that," Adam said. "You don't know anything about this Camille lady. We both saw her looking at my mom's papers. And how she was holding her phone. What else would she have been doing?"

"I don't know. Maybe reading texts. She seemed to check her phone a lot."

Adam shook his head and left the vestibule where we'd just seen Camille out after an uncomfortable and quickened downing of tea and cake. I locked up and followed Adam inside, catching up with him in the kitchen where he was surveying the piles of papers on the table and shaking his head some more.

"That's just great," he said. "The forms right on top are from my mom's company insurance. They show all her personal data." An exhale dragged out from deep in his core.

"Look I know you're upset, but really I don't think this is a problem. I seriously doubt Camille was poking through your mom's stuff." I explained how I'd met Camille and how she'd helped me. "I don't think someone like that is some criminal. She's an investigator, for Pete's sake. She helps stop crimes not commit them."

"An investigator?" Adam said. "What kind of investigator?"

"I don't know exactly. The ordinary kind I guess. She said she helps the police and lawyers and such."

Adam shuffled his mom's loose papers and checked a few of the piles. "Lora, you know my mom worked for a corporate lawyer, right? She was privy to confidential files. Some of these papers are from cases she worked on from home while she was sick."

Adam's mom had had cancer. That's why he'd come home, and me along with him, to help look after her during chemo. She'd had an upturn in her treatment a couple months after we arrived, and she started to work from home part-time until she had enough strength back to return to the office. Her upturn had only lasted a few weeks and then she suddenly went downhill fast, slipped into a brief coma, and died in the hospital soon after. Adam had gone into a kind of shock, functioning on autopilot until the funeral then sinking into grief. But as her only child, sorting her life fell to him. And as his only parent, his dedication to the task hung heavily on his shoulders. The idea that something, or someone, may have compromised his mother in any way understandably hurt and messed with his sense of duty.

And the idea that I may have somehow caused the compromise by letting a stranger into the house, his house, was messing with my own sense of duty. Yet I was still having a hard time buying the idea that Camille was some sort of spy. Especially one interested in Adam's mother or her work. I'd met Camille completely by random, hadn't I? And she had helped me. And she hadn't even laughed me off when I floated the idea of hiring her to find my lost book.

Yes, that was right. I went out to the hall table and picked up a card, Camille's business card. She'd left it on her way out. In case I wanted to get in touch, either for help with my book search or in case I filed a complaint about my purse snatching with the police and needed a witness to add to the report. Unlikely since I got my bag and most of its contents back, but still a nice offer.

I returned to Adam and tapped his arm, busily organizing his mother's papers and stuffing piles into boxes he'd stashed under the kitchen table. He looked at me and I held up the card.

"See," I said softly. "It's okay. Camille left her contact info. Would she have done that if she was snooping on your mother or stealing from us?"

Adam snatched the card and checked first the printed front then flipped it over to where Camille had written an additional phone number on the back. Holding tight to the card, he retrieved his laptop from his bag in the hall, headed towards the living room, and plopped himself onto the couch. Using the coffee table as a desk, he revved on the computer and keyed in something he read off the printed side of the card.

I sat beside him and helped Pong onto the sofa, cradling her by my other side. On Adam's screen, a website for *Investigations C&C* loaded. A photo of the Montréal skyline showing old buildings and plenty of blue sky filled the background, plain menu navigation buttons lining the top. All in French. Adam toggled to the upper corner, clicked EN, and the menu headings converted to English.

"There," I said, pointing to the *"About Us"* section. "Try that."

Adam clicked on it and we each read in silence. I learned the C&C bit of *Investigations C&C* stood for Caron & Caron—Camille's last name and the last name of her brother Laurent, the other investigator listed. His credentials included time on the

Montréal police force while Camille had a whack of investigator certifications. They seemed to jointly own the company and offer an array of services.

Adam sat upright. "This could be anyone. There's no photo. For all we know that business card belongs to someone else."

Oh boy. So now he wasn't just suspicious of Camille snooping on his mom, he wasn't even sure she was legit.

I took a deep breath. Adam had become super protective since his mom died. And I got it. Everyone talks about the five stages of grief—denial, anger, bargaining, depression, and acceptance—but those steps are misleading. They weren't even originally about grief when someone dies at all. They were observations about steps people go through when they face illness. Grief after a loss involves much more. Shock and even guilt sometimes among other things, but also for some fear is a big part—losing a loved one can shake your world, your beliefs, your security. It can be normal to become fearful of more loss, of a lack of control in your life. Or, in Adam's case, fearful of more bad things happening. It was perfectly understandable that he'd become more distrustful and skeptical. Even if that distrust did seem like a leap to me in this case.

I picked up the business card Adam had discarded. "There's one way to find out if it's the same person," I said, carefully, not wanting to sound glib. "I'll call."

Adam ran a hand through his hair. "What will that do? The whole website could be fake."

There was no point me arguing Adam's claim. He knew way more about computers and websites than I did. To my untrained eye, the C&C site looked legit. Probably this was his skepticism talking more than his professional assessment, but pointing any of that out wouldn't ease his concerns.

"Possibly," I said. "But at least the phone numbers match so calling may tell us something." Gently, I eased myself up so as not to disturb Pong, and I went to the kitchen to use the house phone, a portable I brought back with me to the couch.

"Try the printed number, not the one scribbled on the back," Adam told me. "That number isn't anywhere on the site."

Adam flipped through various sections of the website, and I scanned them over his shoulder as I waited for my call to connect.

"*Allô*," a voice said into my ear. Male. Deep. Very French.

"Er, hello," I said. "*Bonjour.* Um. Camille, *s'il-te-plaît?*"

"*Camille?*" The man sounded distracted, like I'd interrupted something far more pressing than answering phones.

"Uh, *oui.*"

"*Camille n'est pas ici. Je peux prendre un message?*"

Message. Message, right. He wanted to take a message. "Um..." My eyes flitted to Adam's computer and the page he'd stopped on, pointing at a section about legal investigations. Oh heck. "Sure," I stammered in English into the phone, giving up on any pretense of holding my own in French with a Frenchman. "Could you please ask her to call Lora."

There was a beat of silence and then the man said, "and your number, Lora?"

Now it was my turn to be distracted. He pronounced the "r" in my name light and feathery, rolling the "r" into the "a." I'd never heard my name like that before, almost lyrical. I resisted the urge to mirror it back, gave him my mobile number, and we said our goodbyes.

Adam's forehead crinkled at me when I set the phone down.

"She wasn't there, was she?" he said.

"Well no. But she didn't leave that long ago. Maybe she had an errand to run on her way to the office." Or maybe she wasn't even going to the office. How did I know? She'd been at the café when I'd met her. Late morning. Maybe this was her day off. Maybe PIs didn't work nine-to-five. Hmm. Unless Adam was right and she was working when I'd met her and our meeting wasn't as random as I thought. I shook my head, letting the thought float by like a cloud. Now I was getting as suspicious as Adam.

The doorbell went, Pong barked, and I automatically checked the old clock on the fireplace mantel, wondering how lunch time could have turned into dinner time so soon. The well-wishers who brought Adam meals had me well trained. I had come to associate the doorbell with food, like a culinary Pavlovian response.

Beside me, Pong flung herself down from the sofa and headed for the front door, tail wagging, mouth slightly panting. At least I wasn't the only one trained. Only this time we were both out of luck. According to the mantle clock, which kept time like a seasoned cook assembles recipes, not quite by exact measure-ments, it was somewhere between two and three in the afternoon. Early yet for dinner deliveries.

Although, possibly it was someone with more cake or maybe cookies. Those could come mid-afternoon.

I strolled out after Pong and Adam, who had edged Pong away from the inner door to make his way out to answer the bell. I scooped up the dog and peered into the vestibule, not making out anybody beyond Adam and not hearing any voices.

"Who is it?" I asked.

Adam bent briefly, stepped back, and closed the door.

"Nobody." He retraced his steps to the hall. "Probably kids playing pranks. Or some lovelorn boy who got the wrong door and chickened out before presenting his crush with this pitiful thing I found sitting on the doormat." Adam held a crumpled carnation out to me, and my mind wheeled back to earlier in the day when I'd stopped by the flower stand en route to my interview. This flower looked a lot like the one I'd used as a bookmark. Albeit a wilted and smushed version.

"Hang on." I dashed around Adam, out the door, and off the porch to the sidewalk, looking up and down the street. In the distance, a man was running. Not some gawky kid. A man. I couldn't quite make him out. It was hard to spot specifics before he rounded the corner, except the hood on his head. A hood much like the one I'd seen on the man who took my purse. Exactly like it in fact. It had to be the same guy. It was too much of a coincidence. A carnation showing up at my door on the same day my book goes AWOL. But why? How did hoodie guy know where I lived? What did he want? And what had he done with my book?

6

"**YOU CAN'T BE** serious."

I matched the intense look Adam leveled at me along with his words. "Of course I'm serious," I told him. "It's the sensible thing to do."

"Sensible? What's sensible about hiring a thief?"

I sighed. "Camille's *not* a thief. And I'm not hiring her." At least not yet. I picked up the portable phone from the coffee table in the living room and I sat on the couch. "I'm just going to ask if she remembers any specifics about the guy who took my book."

Adam settled himself next to me. "And let's say she does. How is that going to help? I hate to say it, but I'm guessing your book is long gone."

"Maybe. But the guy who took it isn't." I explained about my book and the carnation and my suspicions about how the carnation landed on our doorstep, either accidentally or purposefully left by hoodie guy.

Adam pulled the phone from my hands. "Geez, Lora. If the guy who robbed you followed you home, we need to make a police report. For all we know, this Camille is working with the guy. Maybe it's a like a good cop, bad cop, thief routine. One makes a play to rob you, the other pretends to help you and then cases your house after she gains your trust." His gaze flit towards the kitchen. "Or plain out steals from you without you knowing."

The words *"You're concocting theories like that yet question my good sense?"* bubbled in my throat and I tamped them down. Centuries of British ancestry had bestowed me with a stiff upper lip that saved me from many an outburst. And as much as I wanted to be understanding about Adam's post-grief fears, his hypothesis seemed a bit far fetched. I was with him on the concern about hoodie guy, but I trusted my instincts about Camille and something told me she was on the up and up. And I could use her help. While Adam's upset was likely unfounded, mine was very real. My beloved book was gone and the guy who took it just showed up at my door. I couldn't just let that go. Especially if I wanted to get my book back.

I left Adam with the portable and went to get my mobile. It may be last year's model, or maybe even last decade's, but it could still make calls. I dialed the number Camille had scribbled on the back of her business card. The number Adam didn't want to call earlier. Her cellular line I hoped, that went directly to her to save me from chancing a "lost in translation" bit with the Frenchman at her office.

"*Allô*," a voice answered at the other end. Feminine, bright, long draw on the "*A*."

"Um, Camille?"

"*Oui*." Her voice slowed, the tone guarded. Or maybe impatient.

"Hi. It's Lora calling. We met today? At the café?"

"*Ah, oui, oui*." Her inflexion relaxed, street noise in the background, her breathing paced to walking. "How are you? Did you find your book?"

"Actually that's why I'm calling. I didn't. But I wondered if maybe you remembered anything about the guy who took it. He showed up at my house and—"

"*Pardon?* He came to your house?"

"Right."

"He talked to you?" A door slammed after she spoke, background sounds quieted, and something louder whirred on.

"Well, no. I didn't exactly talk to him. He came to the house and ran off. But I think he may still have my book and I thought maybe if I could track him down I could get it back."

"You want to find the man who robbed you and ask him to give back what he stole?"

Okay, when she put it like that it sounded ridiculous. Of course I didn't expect him to just give back my book, more maybe be persuaded to part with it. After all, it was no use to him. But hearing Camille's reaction on top of Adam's had me thinking maybe Adam was right. Not about Camille, but about making a police report. Maybe I was letting my sentimentality about the book fog my judgment. What was I thinking wanting to track hoodie guy down? He was a purse snatcher, a low-life, a book thief, a flower smusher.

Maybe I should worry less about my book and more about some thief knowing where I live. Maybe hoodie guy's visit to the house had nothing to do with my book. Maybe he came expecting to find me alone and got scared off when Adam answered the door.

I moved from the kitchen archway that connected to the dining room, where I'd drifted as I talked on the phone. I could hear Adam coming through from the living room and didn't want him to watch me back-peddle like I was about to do now, lest Camille think I was a complete idiot. "On second thought," I told her. "I think I may just let the police handle it. Really sorry to have bothered you."

"*La police?* Sure." She rattled off the nearest station address where I could go to make a report. "*Probablement* it's good to have a file for when there's more trouble. It helps to have the history for sure."

I moved my mobile to my left ear, the heat of the phone bringing a slight buzz to the right side. "More trouble?"

"*Mais oui.* It's odd, no, the thief coming to your house? He could come again. A man like that who knows what he do. He rob you in the middle of the day at a café. At night under cover of darkness what he do we don't know."

Okay, if Camille was trying to scare me she was succeeding. Between her and Adam, I was beginning to think I could be one step away from some psycho coming at me while I took a shower. Only in my case the psycho would be donning a hood instead of a gray wig.

I released my fingers from the curled grip they'd taken it upon themselves to form around Camille's business card. I straightened the cardboard, easily pliable thanks to my moist palm. I was really in a quandary now. Not just about finding my book but about what to do if hoodie guy did pose a threat. Despite Adam's reservations, it felt wrong to shut things down with Camille just yet. After all, she had seen hoodie guy in action and made a great witness. Also, with her trained eye, she could likely identify him better than even I could and give a better description to the police if I made a report.

I was about to ask her when a long car honk came at me through the phone followed by a string of French words then the call cut out.

"So?" Adam said, coming over to me. "What did she say?"

"Nothing," I said, deliberately downplaying the call, slipping to the hall, and stowing the phone away in my purse. The last thing I needed was to rile Adam's concerns by adding Camille's two cents. My own concerns were rattled enough for both of us.

7

*I*T TOOK SOME convincing to assure Adam I was good. He had a late afternoon meeting, important and tough to cancel at the last minute. "No problem," I'd told him. "Go. I'll be fine."

He wavered.

"Seriously," I'd said. "We don't even know why the guy came or if he'll come back. Probably seeing you scared him off and we'll never hear from him again. Anyway, I'll be in the house with the doors locked and you'll be back in a couple hours. Nothing's going to happen in two hours." For the second time, I kept Camille's comments out of it. No need for Adam to have visions of some shower slasher in his head, too.

Finally Adam relented and left.

Yay me, I thought, bolstered by my own bravado. Much better than letting some purse snatcher dictate our lives. And that's all hoodie guy had proven himself to be so far, I reminded myself. A purse snatcher. Not some psycho killer out to get me.

Alone in the house, I listened to the fridge whirr and the mantel clock tick. Normal house noises. Nothing to be scared of at all.

I looked across the couch at Pong on the far cushion. She wagged her tail and let out a tiny bark which I took as a bark of solidarity. I reached to pat her belly and she barked again, louder, her snout shifting to the bank of windows overlooking the front porch.

"What is it, girl?" I said. "You getting hot?"

Bravado went much farther in a house with locked doors and windows. Tricky on hot summer days in an old house without central air. A lone window air-conditioner gurgled in a room upstairs, keeping the rising heat from scorching levels but offering little help for the first floor. And now that I'd locked the place up tight to keep out hoodie guys that may go bump in the night, the sticky, stale, warm air felt heavy.

"C'mon, Pong," I called, standing and stepping to the hall. "Let's move this show up to the next level and get some heat relief."

Pong jumped off the couch, bypassed the stairs, veered to the vestibule door instead, and scratched at it. A throat tilting bark escaped her when the doorbell sounded mid-scratch.

My pulse quickened. Surely that wasn't hoodie guy. Back so soon? It couldn't be. Maybe Camille?

I tip-toed to the living room windows. My call with Camille *had* ended abruptly, and I had no idea why or what she'd said before she cut out. No online translator could help me decipher words I had no idea how to spell or pronouce. I'd picked up the phone twice to call her back, but I'd been too embarrassed to follow through and ask what she'd said in French before she rang off. Maybe she'd planned to stop by.

Or maybe it was one of Adam's well-wisher meal deliveries. It *was* close to dinner time.

There were lots of visitor possibilities besides hoodie guy, right?

I squeezed myself into the narrow space at the end of the sofa and edged a slip of curtain aside to get a peek at whoever had just pressed my bell again. I made out a tallish figure on the porch, posture strong, physique male, dressed in a dark button shirt and dark jeans. Too young for Adam's mom's friends but not a friend of Adam's I recognized. And obviously not Camille. Possibly hoodie guy minus the hood, my galloping heart suggested?

The man turned from the door front and I stumbled back a few steps to clear his view, banging into a standing lamp, stumbling forward to grab onto it before it fell.

"Lora?" I heard as my forehead grazed the window pane.

I fought the urge to crouch and hide. Whoever it was had seen me. And knew my name.

Pong ran to the window, stretched herself onto her hind legs, and yapped.

"*Allô*, Lora," the voice went again, throaty yet somehow infusing my name with a melodic lilt. I paused, faint memory coming to me as I placed the voice. The Frenchman at Camille's office.

I rubbed at my forehead and went to let him in. Maybe that's what Camille had said in our call, that she was sending over a colleague. Whoever it was had to be better than hoodie guy showing up again.

"Hi," I said, extending my hand to introduce myself when I got to the door.

The Frenchman passed me a card, the same look as Camille's only bearing a different name. Laurent Caron. Her brother and partner listed on the website.

My hand went to the neckline of my dress. Oh boy. Her business partner. Not some junior investigator passing by with a brochure on home security tips. Had I somehow engaged their PI agency during my call with Camille? How would I pay for that? I was living off my savings until I got a job. And what services had I unintentionally agreed to or requested? Finding my book or dealing with hoodie guy? I seriously had to sign up for French courses pronto. I literally couldn't afford theses types of communication snafus.

I closed the door to the outside heat and grimaced at Pong licking the newcomer's hand, her tail in a mad wag. Some guard dog. Not that I blamed her. The man emanated an aroma that reminded me of cinnamon toast. The dog paused her licking, dashed to the living room, and came back with one of her toys and tossed it at the PI's feet.

Oy. That was like the canine welcome wagon. She was making it much harder for me to do what I had to do, which was somehow un-hire the man and send him on his merry way.

"So you're Camille's brother?" I said.

"And you're the *Américaine* from the café."

I looked at him properly for the first time. His dark eyes were partially shielded by dark hair strands swinging free around his face and edging past his chin towards the back. His mouth sat in a relaxed smile surrounded by dark scruff. His shirt was unbuttoned at the collar and rolled at the sleeves, muscular forearms showing dark hair. No watch, no visible tattoos, no wedding band. Surprising since I placed him just a nudge older than me, early thirties maybe, and it was easy to imagine him on the arm of just about any woman walking down the marriage aisle. Harder to imagine him as a PI. Something indefinable about him even my social work training couldn't quite peg. Then again, maybe that made him the perfect PI.

We stood rather close, the tiny foyer barely big enough for one person let alone two and a dog, and my manners took hold.

"Sorry," I said, slipping into the house and gesturing towards the living room. "Come in."

He removed his shoes without a word, added them to the line of mine and Adam's on the floor, and walked through.

I watched him take in the place, his eyes barely moving, yet somehow I had the sense he'd registered not only the approximate age of the house but the value of its contents. And probably more than a little information about the occupants. The first time I'd come to the house, I'd automatically assessed the vintage furniture bought before it turned vintage, the aged wool rug, the faded wallpaper, and the seventies wall art and knickknacks, and I'd known immediately what sort of woman Adam's mom was. At least as far as surroundings can provide. I was guessing Laurent was doing the same appraisal. Occupational hazard, same as me.

Only I wasn't used to being on the receiving end. Not that much of the room gave anything away about me. The only bits in the room belonging to me were Pong and the rocking chair draped in a cotton throw blanket by the fireplace that had gotten me through many a cold Montréal winter night when we'd first arrived.

The lame opening line about Laurent being Camille's brother did belong to me, though. Ugh. That probably came off like dinner party chatter. Not something you say to a professional who appears at your door. Worse, I'd posed it as a question when I knew perfectly well they were siblings. If I hadn't seen it on the website, I'd have known it by looks alone. The similar chiseled bone structure, the athletic build. The alert engagement in their eyes, albeit different shades of brown.

His darker versions settled on me and I felt the full force of their intensity, turning my own eyes away before he read too much and knew how completely lost this day had left me. The failed interview, the book theft, the purse snatcher out there some-where rocking my sense of safe.

The only bright spot had been meeting Camille, and Adam's suspicions of her had tainted that and put me on guard. Especially now as I became very much aware that I'd just let a second stranger into the house. No matter that my instincts told me the siblings were fine people or that Pong's instincts seemed to concur as she sat patiently by Laurent waiting for him to throw the ball she'd just brought him. I knew Adam wasn't comfortable with Camille and his discomfort would likely extend to Laurent.

What I didn't know was a polite way to get the man to leave.

"*Bon ben*. I heard you lost an important book," Laurent said.

I nodded. "It was a gift from my parents."

"*Persuasion?*" he ventured, the name sounding different in his French accent.

I nodded again.

"And you need help to get it back?"

"Well," I paused unsure what to say. I wanted the book back more than anything, but here was that tricky hiring thing again. How could I say yes when I didn't have a job and would have to pay any costs out of the meager savings I was living on? But how could I say no when I wanted help? I really didn't know what to do.

"It's a good story, *Persuasion*," Laurent said before I landed on an answer. "About a girl who loses her love, no? Because she listens to other people's opinions instead of following her heart?"

I perched myself on the edge of the sofa arm. "You know it?" I said, surprised.

He shrugged. "A bit. The name of the heroine is Anne or Andrea or something like that?"

I felt my head tilt slightly. "Anne."

He smiled. "And she lived with her mother and brothers, no?"

"Her father and she had grown up with sisters."

He dipped to retrieve Pong's ball and threw it for her to catch. "*Oui*. I remember now. It's a good story."

"I'm surprised you know it. Camille didn't."

He stayed focused on his game with Pong. "Camille is not much for romance stories."

"And you are?" I said.

He glanced at me. "Some."

"I know it must seem funny to care so much about a lost book. And I know the odds of finding it in a huge city are insanely bad." My words brought a weight to my heart the minute I said them because I knew that last bit was especially true.

Laurent set Pong's ball down on the floor near the rocking chair. "Maybe not as bad as you think."

I brightened. "Really?"

"The man at the table with you at the café. What was his name?"

"The guy who took my purse?"

"No. The other one. The one inside the café."

My neck tingled. How did Laurent know about the man who sat at my table? Camille maybe? Had she seen the guy before I moved to the patio? That had to be it. Probably she saw me inside when she'd gone to get her food.

"I don't know," I said, rising to stand. "He just sat down after me. It was crowded. Why?"

"He had a book, no?" Laurent said, watching me.

"I guess. A journal I think." Laurent didn't need to know I'd spied on the poor man and tried to read his notes. "But the guy at my table didn't take my book. I know because I remember putting it in my bag before I went outside."

"And his book?"

"What about it?"

43

"Where did it go?"

"I don't know." I cocked my head at all the questions, confused how any of this would help me. "I guess he took it when he left." Beside me, Pong came to sit at my feet and cocked her head at Laurent, too. Probably wondering when he'd stop talking and get back to their ball game.

"You guess?"

An odd sensation settled between my shoulders. "You ask a lot of questions," I said.

"*Bon ben.* That's the best way to get answers."

I couldn't tell by his tone if he was serious or playing with me.

Maybe the expression on my face showed my bemusement because he said, "The faster we trace what happened, the better the chances of finding your book. The longer something is gone, the worse the chances of finding it."

"I thought that was missing people."

He shrugged. The same offhand way Camille had of shrugging. "It works for both."

A knock at the front door went and Pong let out a chesty bark and pranced to the entranceway, the skip in her step telling me she was sure it was a food delivery this time.

I opened the door, expecting she'd be right, to find Camille walking through the threshold instead and French words sailing over my head to Laurent. He came back at her with his own barrage of French and I closed the door, trapping their verbal tennis match inside.

They were on either sides of the coffee table when they stopped talking long enough to notice me enter the room. As a look passed between them, I got a sense maybe I had that wrong. Maybe they'd only stopped then because they were talking *about* me and shut their conversation down with me in earshot. Although truth be told, at their volume I'd always been in earshot. As had my neighbors I was sure. Who I was also sure probably understood more than I had. All I'd picked up on was my name, talk about a book, and the mention of some guy called Grégoire.

"*Regarde,*" Camille said quietly, arm swinging towards me but eyes on Laurent. "*T'es satisfait? Elle ne le connait pas.*" Her gaze moved to me. "*Je m'excuse pour mon frère.* My brother shouldn't have bothered you. He will go now."

Laurent leaned against the living room doorframe and crossed his arms over his chest. "I'm not going. You go. We were doing fine before you got here."

"Why?" Camille said, her tone growing higher. "Because she passed your test?"

The "she" had to be me, but what test had I passed? "Test? What test?" I asked.

Camille rolled her eyes. "He wanted to see if you were part of the plan at the café."

Plan? There was a plan?

"You did the same thing this afternoon!" Laurent said.

"*Exactement!* It was done. I told you she was fine but you had to check yourself." She rolled her eyes again. "*On arrête là.* We tell her now."

He shot her a look she waved off before lowering her voice to normal volume and adding, "*Mais voyons,* we have to tell her if we want her to cooperate."

Wow. I was so lost. A plan. A need for me to cooperate in some way. What the heck were they talking about? Did I even want to know? This morning I hadn't even met these people and now they were in my living room talking plans.

"Look," I said. "I'd love to help with whatever this is but, gee, it's getting late and my boyfriend will be home for dinner soon." My boyfriend who would plotz to come home to find not just Camille back again but her brother as well. I waved towards the hall. "Maybe we could pick this up tomorrow?"

The siblings looked at each other then back at me.

"*Non*. Tomorrow is too late," Laurent said.

"I don't think so." I frowned. "Um, too late for what exactly?"

"Too late for you maybe," Camille said. "If the man with the hood comes back."

8

"**S**ERIOUSLY? ESPIONAGE?" I laughed as I tried to get a handle on things when they started to explain. "Me, a spy?" As if. Although at least then I'd have a job. And a catchy job title to boot. I looked at Laurent. "You thought I could be a spy?"

"Why not you?" he said.

On another day I may not take that as a compliment, but today I did. Although it did seem like a lot of spy suspicions had been bandied about what with Adam saying a similar thing earlier about Camille spying on his mom's files. What was with men and all their suspicions about women being spies? Something in the movies maybe? Although Adam at least had more to go on with Camille being a PI and all. That was pretty close to being a spy. Me, on the other hand, had never so much as spied through a keyhole.

"Why would you think I was a spy?" I asked Laurent.

"Not a spy exactly. A contact. You met Grégoire at the café. On your own with a book and a flower. That was the signal."

I laughed again. "You guys are making this up. This has to be a joke. Spies don't meet in cafés. These days, they probably meet in offices. Or ping each other by encrypted email or text messages. They absolutely don't carry books with flowers for bookmarks."

"They do when they pass information they hide in books," Camille said. "Electronic communication can be traced. Books not so easy. And books are easier to destroy after without leaving a trail."

I checked her face and then Laurent's. Both deadly serious. Then I thought about hoodie guy taking my purse but only pinching the book. Leaving all the money and credit cards.

Oh my. Maybe spies do pass around books with flowers. And some spy thinks my book has some kind of secret message. Now how would I get the book back? And if I did, in what condition? What would they do to it before they realized they had the wrong book? Or worse, what if they already did realize and had sent hoodie guy around to get the right book? What if they thought I was holding out on them or pulled some kind of switch? That couldn't be good.

"No," I said, as much to myself as to Camille and Laurent. "This is too ridiculous."

They were both seated on the couch, Camille leaning back, Laurent leaning forward, his forearms on his knees, his dark hair obscuring his eyes. Each periodically fanning their clothes away from their bodies, probably to fend off the muggy air in the room. Neither said anything to contradict me.

"Just what kind of spies are these people then?" I asked. "International sleepers, drug traffickers, inside traders?"

"Inside traders and traffickers aren't spies," Camille corrected. "*Peut-être des* sleepers."

"Whatever," I said. "What do these spies do?" I tried to remember to breathe, bracing myself. I couldn't bear to think of some seedy low-life with his grubby hands on my beloved book. "What information were they passing?"

"*Des recettes,*" Laurent said, his voice low, deepening its gravelly tone and making it tough to make out.

"Excuse me?" I said. "Sorry, were you speaking English or French? I'm not so great with French yet."

Camille nodded agreement, like she'd already filed away my limited language skills. "He meant recipes."

I couldn't have heard that right. "Recipes?" I giggled trying to get the next words out. "So these are recipe spies?"

"Corporate spies," Laurent clarified. "Corporate espionage is very serious. The man you saw at the café is passing recipes from a local *chocolatière* to a conglomerate. The *chocolatière* invented a new exclusive line. It's a huge investment for her. To have her recipes stolen, copied, and made by someone else could put her out of business. With their scale of production and distribution channels, the big company can produce the chocolate much cheaper. She won't be able to keep up and she can't afford the time or money for court battles to prove they stole from her. Her store would be bankrupt long before things got settled."

Okay, that did sound bad. But it was still a little funny. The idea of spies dealing in chocolate secrets. And I didn't see why it couldn't wait a day. I mean even if hoodie guy came back, what was he going to do to me? Force feed me ganache? Or if he did sneak up on me in the shower, what? Fill my shower head with liquid chocolate and encase my body like a bon bon?

"So these spies are dealing in chocolate?" I smiled despite my best efforts to hold it in. "And this Grégoire guy at my table had some *chocolatière's* secret recipes in his notebook. Just how did he get these recipes?"

"He used to work for her."

Ah. Okay, made sense. Disgruntled employee maybe. Or

opportunist looking to sell her out and make bank on the side. "And that guy who took my purse? He was the spy?"

"*Non.* Grégoire at your table had the recipes. His contact, it appears didn't show," Laurent explained, locking eyes with me until it felt like he'd seen clear through me, and I had the sudden urge to confess I really was a corporate spy and had been at the café to pick up hush hush recipes for one-of-a-kind, out of this world truffles or something.

"So who was hoodie guy then?"

A glance passed from Camille to Laurent and they both shrugged.

"Hoodie guy?" Camille said.

"Right." I nodded. "The guy wearing the hoodie who took my purse."

"*Ah, oui,*" she said. "That's the problem. We don't know. *Proba-blement* he works for another competitor. Or he was hired by them to take the book."

Hmm. Color me confused. *Probablement* aka probably?

"It's about distance," Laurent added. "Corporate espionage is not always direct. Sometimes a company prefers to hire a go-between."

I was starting to get it. "So then the go-between does the actual stealing and the company stays disconnected from the source."

"*Exactement,*" Camille said.

"But you said probably, right? Probably hoodie guy works for this go-between? Maybe for another company that wants to steal the recipes?"

"*Oui.*"

I frowned. "You're not sure?"

Camille shook her head. "It's not like these thieves-for-hire have an employee listing page *en ligne.*"

No, of course not. Another thought occurred to me and my

frown deepened. "But whoever he is, hoodie guy was after the book and he did come to my house, so there's a good chance he thinks I was Grégoire's contact and that I still have what he wants. Like he just got the wrong book or something."

Camille nodded.

"But I don't have anything," I went on. "I have no idea what happened to Grégoire's book. Or to the no-show contact."

"Neither do we," Camille said. "We're looking into that also. It's obvious to us now that you were not the contact so you would be out of it except—"

"Except hoodie guy obviously still thinks I'm involved or he wouldn't have come to my house," I finished for her.

Camille waved a hand in the air. "*C'est ça.*"

"And since you don't know who he is or how to find him but you want to so you can find out how he figures in, I'm the link, right?"

Camille nodded. "When he comes back, we want you to give him this." She pulled a small diary from the bag slung over her shoulder.

She placed the diary in my hands and I blinked at it, something about the giant sunflower on the cover twigging at me. I'd seen that sunflower recently. Very recently. The wheels of my mind churning to remember where. Oh, that was it. Wheels. There'd been a book with a sunflower just like this one in the toy basket below the seat of the stroller that had bumped my table at the café. The stroller with the mom and two kids. Beside the coloring book the mom had pulled out for her daughter, I'd seen a small book emblazoned with sunflowers. Was this the same one? And if so, how did it get from the café to my living room?

9

"*L*ET ME GET this straight," I said. "You weren't hired to stop the recipe thief or catch him in the act. You were hired to swap his book for this?"

"*Ben*, the plans of our client are private," Laurent said.

Camille's foot tapping grew louder. She'd moved and now stood by the fireplace, flicking Pong's ball up and down in her palm like a reverse yo-yo, seemingly unconcerned with Pong's eyes following the ball's every move from mere inches from Camille's feet.

"*Voyons*, Laurent," she told him. "*Le plan n'est pas un secret d'état.*" Then to me she added, "that's part of it, yes. Even if we caught Grégoire passing along the book of recipes, we would have no authority to stop him. We couldn't prove his intent in that instant. It was easier to switch the book instead and stop the recipes from moving on to the corporation buying them."

"Isn't that like entrapment or something?"

She shook her head. "*Non, non.* We were not baiting anyone. It's them who make the meeting. And switching the book is not like planting evidence. Our book is benign."

I tapped the sunflower diary. "But it's also got recipes, right? Just not the real ones?"

She nodded.

"And the mom with the stroller works for you?"

"Sometimes. When she's not at school. She's our *cousine*, Arielle, still taking her degree."

"Wow," I said, impressed. "A college student with a part-time job and two little kids. That's a lot."

"*Non non*," Camille said. "The kids are not hers. They belong to another cousin. But good props, no? If Arielle could have made the book switch, the plan would have worked magnificently. *Mais* she was late and the only book she saw was yours, and you grabbed it away too fast. I was waiting outside to follow the contact after the switch, and when I saw the problem I was going to get this one from her and swap it for yours outside, but the man with the hood got to you first. Useless for us anyway if your book was not the right one, but we didn't know that then."

Hmm. Seems everyone thought I'd somehow gotten hold of Grégoire's book or that we'd swapped books. And all because he sat at my table. I had to hand it to their cousin Arielle, though. She'd done an excellent job in her role as the mom even if she had mistaken me for a spy.

"And now it looks like two different people want the recipe book," I said. "Whoever Grégoire was supposed to meet and whoever hoodie guy works for. You know the contact works for the big company, but you have no idea who hoodie guy works for or where Grégoire's book went. All we know for sure is that my book is missing and hoodie guy knows where I live and may think I've got what everyone wants. And so if he does approach me again, you want me to give him this fake book, the one you were going to switch for Grégoire's before you knew a second recipe thief was involved."

"*Oui.*"

I shook my head, trying to take it all in. "Wow. This is not how I expected my day to go today. Who knew there could be all this fuss over a little chocolate?"

Camille smiled. "*Mais alors*, not just any *chocolat.*" She dropped Pong's ball into the rocking chair, rummaged in her bag again, and came out with a small rectangular pink box with tiny white polka dots. She lifted the lid off the box and a delicate sweet aroma wafted out like mist from a genie escaping a bottle. She brought the box closer in offering, and I spied three perfect squares of chocolate, each cushioned in pale pink miniature cupcake-style wrappers.

I ditched the diary and picked out the chocolate closest to me, decorated with a delicate rose of icing on top. I took a tentative bite and my tongue was splashed with the essence of what I imagined a rose would taste like if it was kissed by warm sun and bathed in dark chocolate in exact equal degrees. "My goodness. This is amazing."

Camille smiled some more. "*Oui. Vraiment* good, right?"

I finished it and went in for a second, nodding. "I'm no chocolate connoisseur, but I can totally see someone stealing the recipe for these. These could be the secret to world peace. Pass these out to everyone and they'd be too happy to fight with each other."

Laurent's arm grazed mine and beat me to the last shiny, square mound in the box. Our eyes locked and he paused and toggled the confection in his fingers.

"Were you wanting this one also?" He stilled his hand and let the chocolate rest in his upturned palm like it was a dessert platter. "You can have it. I thought you were done."

I pried my gaze from the chocolate. "No, no. You go ahead."

He polished it off and Camille tossed the box on the coffee table next to where I'd set the diary. I picked up the diary and gave it a onceover. It had a flimsy lock on the side, combination style, that rattled but didn't open when I tried it.

"I don't think the notebook the man at my table had with him had a lock," I said. "I think it was more like a journal than a diary. And now that I think about it, I don't think it had a design on it. I'm pretty sure it was a solid color." Possibly blue like my Jane Austen, but I could be remembering that wrong, projecting because the two books had been mistaken for each other. "But let's say I do pass this along to hoodie guy if he shows up, and I'm just saying *if*," I accentuated, "he might peg this as a fake straight off and know I'm bluffing him." Hoodie guy may have no idea what Grégoire's book looked like, but if he did and called me on it I'd be sunk.

"You'll be fine." Laurent took the diary from me, fiddled with it using some doodad he'd pulled from his pocket, and the lock popped open.

"No, seriously," I said. "I'm a terrible liar. I can only tell white lies. I can't bluff. When I was in high school I once tried to play the secret murder card game with friends at a pajama party and I flew into a fit of giggles when the "murderer" winked at me in secret. The game was over then and there. I woke up with my underwear in the freezer."

Laurent's eyes swung to Camille.

"*C'est une blague*," she told him. "A girl thing."

A second more fiddling and Laurent replaced the diary in my hands. The tiny book's sides now free of any signs of a lock. Nothing left but barely perceptible pinholes lost in speckled sunflower images where the lock had attached.

I smiled at him. "Better." Sunflower image not withstanding that was. I thumbed through the pages, some filled, some not. The filled ones had French notes centered on the pages, doodle-like sketches of fancy chocolates on facing pages, the occasional smear of chocolate here and there. I couldn't vouch for the ingredients, of course, since I couldn't even read most of them, but it was easy to imagine the notes belonging to a *chocolatière*.

Something stirred in me, a gnawing starting in my toes and working its way up. The very idea of some faceless conglomerate, maybe even two, taking advantage of a talented *chocolatière* just trying her best to make a go of her trade. I didn't know a lot about the chocolate business, but I was guessing it took a lot of time and care to create specialty confections like the one I'd devoured with the sweet pink rose on top. And that was just one of many she'd created. A lot of trial and error probably went into her inventions. Years of perfecting skills and refining ingredients. The *chocolatière* Camille and Laurent were trying to help had earned her way and a chance to make a go of her business. Nobody should be able to mess with that.

"Okay," I said. "I'll do it."

"*Bien*," Camille said. "Just one more little thing." She took the journal from me and bent it on its spine. "Don't let your hoodie guy see this."

I peered into the curved opening formed at the bend. A thin rectangular slip of white sat partway down from the top. Looked like white plastic or metal. "What is it?" I asked.

She waved her hand in the air dismissively. "*Rien. Un truc.* Like the thing they put in clothes at the store to make the alarm go if someone leaves without paying."

"Like an anti-theft device?"

"Pretty much."

The siblings eyes met and Camille said no more.

"C'mon," I said, having none of that. "If I'm going to help, I should know exactly what I'm helping with, shouldn't I? What else does it do?"

"It will track the location of the book," Laurent said.

"Ah. You mean it will help track hoodie guy when he takes the book back to whoever's waiting for it." I looked at each of them in turn.

Two blank faces looked back at me. The tick tock of the mantel clock beyond them underscoring their silence. Followed almost immediately by the sound of a flicking coin being tossed in the air between them and landing on Camille's forearm. Her mouth twitched and she pocketed the coin, hoisted her mini-pack more securely onto her shoulder, and moved to the hall.

This was good. If they weren't going to bother answering my question, at least they were leaving. According to the mantel clock, Adam would be home any minute or fifteen or so now. Much better they be gone before he arrived.

"Fine," I said. "Have it your way." I started after Camille for the foyer. "I'll call once I pass this phony book along if hoodie guy shows up."

I turned, expecting Laurent to be behind me. He sat on the couch, thumbing through a coffee table book of impressionist art.

My eyes darted to Camille fastening her boots then back to Laurent. "Um. Aren't you going with Camille?" I asked him.

Camille rolled her eyes. "We had a coin toss. He's staying."

Heat rushed to my face. "Staying." Oh no. "Why? He can't stay."

"*Oui*," Laurent said from the couch. "We can't ask you to do this and take risks by yourself. It's not right. I stay. Make sure you're safe. We don't know who the man with the hood is or what he will do when he comes."

Oy. At this moment, I was less concerned with what hoodie guy would do than what Adam would do if he came home to find not just another stranger in his house, but a man dressed in enough black to make John Wayne nervous and the outline of what looked like a gun bulging at his ankle.

10

"*H*E'S HERE," I said, backing away from the living room curtains, fanning my hands in front of me, ordering my shoulders to stand down.

Laurent slipped fast and silent from the living room couch through the archway to the dining room, the softest of breezes passing me in his wake, moving like a panther stealthily escaping into the night.

"Wait until he knocks and the dog barks," Laurent said. "Then answer and be calm. Don't let him see the dog, leave her outside the foyer door and let her to bark, let him imagine her bigger than she is."

"Imagine?" I said. "He doesn't have to imagine how big the dog is. He lives with her for goodness sake." I craned my neck to keep Laurent in view around the bend of wall that separated the living room and dining room. "What are you doing in there? You can't stay there. Come back to the couch." I scanned the area. "No, wait, not the couch, the chair by the fireplace." I went to the sofa. "I'll be on the couch, you be on the chair in the corner." Yes, the corner was good. Contained and far from any personal papers or anything remotely interesting to a snoop. "Hurry," I said when Laurent didn't budge.

"Didn't you just say the man with the hood is here?" Laurent whispered.

I rolled my eyes. "Not him. Adam. Adam's home and he can't find you in the dining room." It was bad enough Laurent was in the house, let alone wandering about. I pointed at the corner chair and felt my eyes pinch. "Please, go sit."

Laurent moved to the archway. "Adam? *C'est ton chum?*"

"Adam's my boyfriend," I told him, having no idea what he asked but knowing it had something to do with Adam. Then hearing a key in the lock, I waved at Laurent to stop talking and sit already.

Which he did. Promptly. Beside me on the sofa, his perusal of the art book resumed before his butt hit the cushion, his breathing as relaxed and slow as if he hadn't moved for hours.

"I come bearing pizza," Adam said, appearing in the doorway. His hands held tight to a massive square box as his foot reached behind him to ease the vestibule door closed while Pong danced on her hind legs in circles around him, projecting her nose as high as it could reach in the direction of the pizza.

I sprang up and over to the hall to relieve him of the box. "We have a visitor," I blurted. "This is Camille's brother, er, Laurent." I shuffled the box from Laurent's direction back to Adam's. "And this is Adam." Not the best introduction but a better pre-empt than when I'd introduced Camille.

The men exchanged slight chin nods, and Adam went to shake Laurent's hand with a formality more suited to a business meeting than a casual meet and greet. Laurent was standing now, the art book crooked in one arm, the other accepting Adam's handshake.

"Laurent came over to, uh, give Camille a ride home," I

explained. "She forgot something here before and came by to get it."

Adam's head moved in a scan of the room.

"Oh, she's not here anymore," I said, flushing. "They got their signals crossed."

Laurent shot me a look and I shot him a "see, I told you I'm a pitiful liar" look back.

"Lora tells me you make video games," Laurent said to Adam.

"What? Oh yeah, I do. Well, I make educational games for kids they can play on the computer at school or home or whatever."

"*Bon ben.* Maybe I get the names. I have young cousins that probably play them at school. They be impressed that I meet you."

"Oh, that's a great idea," I said, knowing full well I'd never said anything to Laurent about Adam's work, figuring it was another tidbit passed on by Camille. "You can stay for dinner and Adam can tell you all about his games." I joggled the pizza box. "We've got plenty of pizza. You like pizza?"

I smiled as brightly as I could without verging on lunatic territory. Adam's face had a "deer in headlights" look and I felt guilty about not telling him the truth about Laurent straight away. I meant to but the excuse about Camille came out first. I wasn't sure why. I'd never bent the truth with Adam before. If he hadn't been so touchy lately and already suspicious of Camille, I probably would have told him everything when he walked through the door. But I didn't want to trigger another upset related to his mom and his protection of her. I was trying to spare his feelings and just needed time to think of a way to explain about Laurent and hoodie guy's possible return that wouldn't rile Adam.

Plus, technically I was helping PIs with a case. I didn't know if I could talk about that. As a social worker, I understood about client confidentiality and knew all about the rules and regulations when it came to privacy laws. I had no idea how those applied to PI work. My first instinct always went to need-to-know status, but the lines blurred with this situation.

Laurent set the art book down on the coffee table. "Sure. Pizza would be good. Nice of you to invite me."

"All right then," Adam said and ran a hand through his hair, flashing a searching gaze my way. "I'll just nip upstairs a sec and be right back."

When Adam had gone, Laurent didn't even ask me about where I'd come up with the excuse about him being here to fetch Camille. Like my flimsy fabrication was nothing and his stepping in with a topic change that swept right over my fib was par for the course. Ditto my trying to cover the real reason for his presence in the house with a dinner invite. He seemed to take it all in stride. Like we were partners performing a bit we did every day. No big deal. The same way Camille had shrugged off her chasing of hoodie guy after my purse snatching.

Which got me wondering just who were these two siblings I was letting into my life. And how in the world I'd explain to Adam the deal I'd made to help them with the *chocolatière* book switch plan.

11

I DECIDED IT was best to come clean. Just as soon as Adam was done showing Laurent his video games. I'd cut cucumber spears and carrot sticks to go along with the pizza, and we'd eaten in the dining room under a haze of tension and a steady stream of conversation that Laurent spurred on whenever it lagged. Covering everything from local happenings to hockey to music but always circling back to Adam and his work.

Mostly I listened. I wanted to keep myself from blurting something awkward, but I'd also gotten caught up in admiration for Laurent's technique. He drew Adam out in much the same way I'd been trained to deal with reluctant social work clients, the sort who were ordered to attend counseling or dragged along by a spouse or family member. There were techniques to help ease wariness and build sharing. Techniques I was guessing cops learned as well because Laurent seamlessly wove them into his part of the conversation, so well that without my own training I never would have spotted them. And so well Adam didn't seem to notice and was almost cheery when he'd set up his laptop in the living room to demonstrate some of the games he'd designed. Handy for me because it bought me more time to figure out how to explain how Laurent had gone from perfect stranger to dinner guest in a mere few hours.

I finished loading the dishwasher, gave the dog her backyard trot, and filled her bowls with fresh water and dog crunchies. I tidied the tea towels and wiped the counters. I rearranged the flowers Adam had brought me and washed out the kettle. Some of the boxes of papers under the kitchen table were askew, so I slid them into a tighter fit. It was when I found myself contemplating alphabetizing the spices and refilling the straw dispenser that I realized I was almost literally grasping at straws to avoid facing Adam. Not like me at all. I never hedged on difficult tasks. And this didn't even qualify as difficult. This was just me doing a favor for someone who had helped me. A quid pro quo kind of thing really. Nothing more, nothing less.

I took a deep breath and marched myself towards the living room, stopping short at the sound of a faint knock at the front door.

Laurent looked from the computer screen to me when I loitered at the vestibule, his gaze a reminder that maybe there was a tad more than quid pro quo involved in the evening's agenda. His deeming it necessary to remain on the premises already proof enough of that.

"Will you get that, hon?" Adam said, his focus still glued to his laptop on the coffee table.

I took another deep breath and picked up the sunflower book from where I'd stowed it on the antique washstand serving as drop central in the hallway. I slipped into the vestibule, leaving Pong pacing in the hall, remembering Laurent's advice to keep her out of sight. I held the book behind my back in one hand and opened the door with the other.

Under the faint glow of the porch light mixing with late day dusk stood Camille, dressed completely in black, a small black valise at her side.

"I'm here to relieve my brother," she said, moving forward to enter.

Mixed emotions went through me. Relief that it wasn't hoodie guy and alarm that Camille had brought a valise.

She set it down while she removed her shoes and I locked up.

"*Bonjour tout le monde,*" she said when we passed into the house.

Laurent smiled at her. "You're back."

"*Bien sûr.* He's not here yet and you're not staying all night." She patted her suitcase. "That's my job."

At the sight of Camille, Adam pecked at his computer keys and flipped the lid down. "Who's not here? And what's this about someone staying the night?"

Camille raised an eyebrow at me. A ball's-in-your-court eyebrow.

I plunged in and told Adam about my quid pro quo helping of Camille, and by extension Laurent and the *chocolatière*. I kept it brief, my involvement low key. As I went, I paused here and there, looking for cues that I was sharing too much about the case, but neither sibling stopped me at any point. Probably because my version played up the mistaken identity thing that led to my purse snatching and the loss of my beloved book more so than the recipe switch-to-come part.

Adam stood when I was done. "Can I talk to you in the kitchen?"

He walked out of the room before I could answer, and I excused myself and went to join him.

"No," he said when I got to where he'd stopped in the farthest corner of the kitchen, next to the door to the sunroom.

"No?"

"No. This is a bad idea. Give them back whatever it is of theirs you've got and ask them to leave."

I shook my head. "I'm sorry, Adam, but I'm not doing that. I might be able to help these people and that's what I'm going to do. Besides, this way I may get my book back." I hadn't quite worked out how yet, but the possibility had been hovering in my brain. Like maybe if I actually got to talk to hoodie guy I could convince him to return my book. Maybe in exchange for the sunflower book like we were making a trade.

Adam let out a sigh. "You're not going to get your book back. Whoever took it doesn't care about your book. He probably tossed it already. You're talking about some two-bit kid hired to nab a book. Most of the time he probably picks pockets or steals purses or shopping bags or whatever. This is nothing but another job to him. All he's interested in is getting whatever he was hired to steal into the right hands so he can keep all his fingers."

"So? What's your point? Then I'd be helping him keep his fingers, too. That's not a bad thing." After all, hoodie guy couldn't be held responsible for bringing in a fake recipe book. A recipe book was a recipe book. He would have no way of knowing if it was fake or authentic. He'd still be making good on his end of the deal with whoever hired him. Not that I believed hoodie guy's fingers were really in jeopardy, but I didn't wish trouble on anybody.

Adam stared at me like he was gauging whether or not I'd lost my marbles. Finally, he held up his arms in the surrender position. "Fine. Go ahead. But don't be too disappointed when you don't get your book back. And try to keep all *your* fingers, will you?"

I smiled. Adam could be a grizzly when trying to be protective, but inside he was really a teddy bear. Still, lucky for me Camille had shown up when she did. Even a teddy bear may have qualms about Laurent as a sleepover guest. Laurent had been uncooperative enough about the seating arrangements with me earlier on the sofa. Something told me, he'd be even more trouble at a pajama party.

"**OH MY GOODNESS**, stop, shush, we're going to wake Adam." I muffled my giggles and darted a look towards the sliver of staircase I could see from where I sat cross-legged in the rocking chair by the fireplace in the living room. All clear. No light switching on. No Adam.

"You did not just say that!" I went on. "There's no way you saw them doing that! They're celebrities for goodness sake. They're not going to just let loose anywhere. And definitely not doing that."

Camille nodded and crossed her heart. "*Je te jure.*" With her free hand, she topped up her drink from a thermos at her side. "*Oh, excuse*, I mean, yes I swear. At a party at a Queen E hotel suite when I went to get my coat from the bedroom. They were there for anyone to see."

I shook my head and stifled more laughs. "You have the funniest stories. You've got to stop. I should go upstairs and let you get some sleep."

Camille's eyes drifted to the mantel clock. "It's only two o'clock."

"Oh, don't trust that old thing," I told her. "It doesn't work right."

She shrugged. "Anyway, you go up. I stay here and keep watch."

I'd offered Camille the sofa bed in Adam's old room, but she'd declined and set up the couch instead. She lounged on it, thermos tucked on one side of her, box of truffles on the other. Both having come from her valise, which turned out to be stocked with very few clothes or toiletries. She'd offered to share from both the box and the thermos, and I was two cups in before I realized the thermos brew was espresso. Even though I'd diluted cup number three by adding big scoops of ice cream, the chance of sleep for me any time soon was slim. The chance of my eyes remembering how to close was still iffy.

"You know," I said, dragging over an ottoman with my leg, propping my feet up, and snuggling under my throw blanket, thankful the night had taken an edge off the day's heat and the AC upstairs streaming down was enough to make the room bearable again. "I know we're waiting around for some creep to pick up something he has no business to and pass it on to someone else who has no right to have it, but I'm having the best time. I haven't laughed like this in ages."

Totally true. Partly of course from the circumstances with Adam's mom, but also because it had been a long time since I'd had a night of girl talk. Back in New York, my closest friends growing up had moved on to lives in different directions, and with working and meeting Adam and all, making new friends had slipped on my priority list. Some co-workers and I had been on acquaintance status but meeting someone I really clicked with just hadn't happened. Once you grew up, making new friends somehow seemed more challenging.

"*Oui. Moi non plus*," Camille said. "You're a very interesting girl, Lora Weaver. To come here to a new city where you don't even speak the language is either brave or—"

Her sentence stopped there hanging in the air.

"Foolish?" I said. And we both laughed. Coffee or not, I recognized overtired laughter when I heard it. I was sure half the things we'd said wouldn't seem near as funny in the morning, but for now we were hilarious.

"But you," I said. "You must have oodles of people to have fun with."

She raised an eyebrow. She did that a lot I was learning.

"Like that guy you lived with?" I said. "Luc? And I'm sure you've got loads of friends."

She smiled and stretched. "Luc, yes, Luc can be very fun. Friends not so much. Like you, they move away. They get married, they have kids. Life gets busy."

I nodded. I heard her on that. "At least you have a brother. With my parents gone, I'm pretty much on my own. I have some relatives on my mom's side in the UK but not many and not any I really know. You seem to have quite a few cousins, and you and Laurent must be pretty close to work together like you do." I shifted position and yawned. "Must be nice."

She closed her eyes and rested her arms across her stomach. "Laurent is two years older. He went to school before me. He drove a car before me. He moved out before me. He likes to play big brother and drive me crazy." She opened one eye. "*Mais* also he was a very good cop and is now a better investigator. So he's a very good partner. But if you tell him I said so, I'll deny it of course."

I smiled. "Of course."

And on that we must have both fallen asleep because the next thing I remember is waking up in the rocker, my legs propped on the ottoman, and dawn light streaming through a crack in the curtains. Alone. The sofa empty of blankets or bodies. Making me wonder if I'd dreamed the whole previous day.

12

PONG STROLLED IN from the direction of the kitchen, licking her lips, tail wagging. I fixed my bleary eyes on her. Dawn was early for her to be up and about. Usually she could be found tucked up in one of her dog beds at this hour or, on cold winter nights, curled up tight on the people bed, having crept on in the night.

I slid out of the rocker, slowly making my way to the kitchen, crossing my fingers that she hadn't found an uninvited playmate. Amid all the charms inherited from a vintage house, critters that considered themselves to have squatters rights was not one of them.

No mini footprints or little "gifts" or other telltale critter signs that I could see, thank goodness. I checked Pong's bowl and found it empty. So gleaming clean I could see my reflection. Yikes. Not pretty. I needed a shower and maybe ten minutes with tea bags draped over the puffy half-moon mutants under my eyes.

I went to the fridge in search of an injection of vitamin C and found a note stuck to the door. I squinted at the words, not recognizing the handwriting, and scanned to the bottom looking for a signature. Camille. I smiled. At least that meant the previous day hadn't been a dream.

The note said she'd been called away during the wee hours and expected to be back around ten. She'd grabbed a bagel on her way out and given Pong a bowl of milk and hoped that was okay.

I looked over at Pong who had straggled in and sat by her bowl, eyes beaming bright.

"Clever girl," I said to her. "You wheedled milk out of our guest. But don't push it. You know you're not supposed to drink milk."

I padded back to the living room, pinched my blanket from the rocker, and went to the sofa to eek out a few more hours of sleep. I had plenty of time before ten and with any luck a few more winks just might reduce my puffy eyes to human sized again.

NO SUCH LUCK. Puffy eyes remained long after my forty winks. Even after I'd swiped an edge of towel over the bathroom mirror, clearing steam from my shower for a better look. The mutants were still there.

"I'm leaving," Adam called out from downstairs.

I ambled out to the hallway in my bathrobe and leaned over the banister. "Okay," I said. "Have a good day." I added in a small wave and a smile to compensate for my groggy, espresso hangover voice.

Adam stood at the bottom of the staircase. He was dressed in tan pants and a red shirt accessorized by his messenger bag and a grimace. "You sure Camille is coming back? If I can't talk you out of this cockamamie plan, maybe I should stick around."

I smiled some more and didn't bother to move the chunk of hair that fell across my cheek, hoping it helped mask my eye bags. Adam hadn't said anything about my late night, but I knew he must have noticed my side of the bed was empty when he got up, and it probably wasn't helping his mood.

"No worries," I told him. "I'm feeling good. I'm not afraid of hoodie guy. If he shows up, I give him the recipe book and he goes away. Easy peasy."

Adam set his bag down. "That's it, I'm staying."

"But I just told you I'm not afraid. I'm not sure I'll get my book back and that stinks, but I'm not afraid."

"Exactly," Adam said, starting up the stairs. "That's why I'm staying. Because you should be afraid. You have no idea what you've let yourself in for and you know nothing about your new friends." He did air quotes around the word friends when he spoke.

I tried not to roll my eyes. "Don't be such a worrywart."

He pulled me to him when he reached me. "When it comes to you, it's my job to be a worrywart. You wouldn't even have been at that café to get into this mess if it wasn't for me. And I know you're down about your career not going so well here yet."

I eased him away enough to look him in the eyes. "Is that what you think? You think I'm doing this because I don't have a new job yet?"

"Kinda."

I crossed my arms over my chest. "I'm not doing this because I'm bored if that's what you think. I'm doing this because helping is the right thing to do. And because it might just get my book back. If it doesn't I'll live with that, but at least I'll know I tried something."

"Fair enough," he said. "But I'm still staying." He moved past me to his old bedroom that he'd been using as a home office since we'd taken over the house. His work had a cyclical nature with times he hunkered down for periods and worked solo, then other times he was out with this team or that, doing demos of his work, or travelling for conferences and such. His current project was in team stage. I knew that. And he knew I knew.

"Suit yourself," I said, returning to the bathroom to finish putting myself together for the day. I sensed there was more to Adam's determination to stick around, but I couldn't put my finger on it yet so I chose not to challenge him. There was only so much a gal could take on before breakfast.

I had thrown on a blue sundress and a touch of makeup, had my hair in a high pony tail, and I was finishing off a bagel at the dining room table when Adam came in. He had his computer bag with him and his car fob in his hand.

"Change your mind about staying home?" I said.

"Not me. My team had a crisis. I've got to go in for a few hours. But I'll have my phone with me. Call when all this business is over so I know you're okay."

"Okey dokey."

He planted a kiss on me, turned to go, and pivoted back around.

"On second thought, call me even if nothing happens," he said.

I smiled. "Sure. I'll call with an update in about an hour or two. But nothing's going to happen. Whether hoodie guy shows or not, I can take care of myself. You forget I'm a trained social worker. I know how to handle myself."

"There's a big difference between handling yourself with some kid in juvie or living in a box on the street than with some kid in the midst of a theft gone bad who has to make good or answer to someone higher up the crime chain."

I had the urge to make a face or a quick comeback but called on my lip-holding superpower to avoid getting into a tangle. My efforts to show patience and understanding during Adam's grief aftermath only went so far. I appreciated his concern about me, but I was starting to see a pattern that idled dangerously close to questioning my judgment. Probably he didn't mean to, I assured myself. Probably it was his genuine concern running amuck.

When he'd left, I took my dishes out to the sink and checked the stove clock. Twenty to ten. Just enough time to take Pong for a short walk around the block before Camille was due to arrive.

Pong did a happy dance when she saw me go for her leash. Walks were hit and miss during heat wave times. Early morning walks before the day grew too hot sometimes worked, but sometimes the humidex kyboshed even those and she was limited to backyard trots, so the happy dance was understandable. She was clipped and ready to go so fast I barely had time to get my sneakers on.

Outside, the sun was already warming the sidewalks like a fry pan readying to cook pancakes. I tried to get Pong around the block at a pace slow enough to keep her from overworking and swift enough to keep her little paws moving before the sidewalk temperature reached bouncing water ball stage. Hot sidewalks could be dangerous for little paws, but luckily Adam's old neighborhood also had massive old trees with leaves like canopies, shielding stretches of walkways here and there from sun reaching cement to give Pong mini breaks.

We got back to the house to find a note taped to the front door. Handwritten in a scrawl and faded in parts, like it was written on the vertical. *Sorry I missed you*, it said. Then something about the café and noon. Initial signature scribbled at the bottom.

"Hmm," I said to Pong as we made our way inside and I washed up and passed her a treat. "Looks like Camille came and went and wants to meet again at the café. At least I think that's what she means."

I fetched my cell phone, dialed Camille, and got voicemail. Not handy for confirming the note details, so I left a message telling her I was on my way and clicked off. I looked out the kitchen window at the detached garage to the rear of the driveway. My Mini was in the garage along with a few other things I'd brought with me and stored when Adam and I had decided to stay on after his mom passed. I didn't drive a lot back in New York, but the Mini was my one big asset. So far, I mostly left my asset in the garage because Montréal traffic and the cost and complications of parking made it easier to take the métro. Today may be an exception, though. Today it felt smarter to take my own car rather than be out in the open since I didn't know where or when hoodie guy may show.

I was halfway to the café in Vieux Montréal when I heard my phone chirp in my purse. My knuckles were white on the steering wheel and my sundress clung to my thighs with sweat, a combination of driving anxiety and heat. No way could I get to my phone to answer even if I didn't follow the "no phone while driving" laws. Which I did, and I didn't have an ear bud and wasn't sure my clunker phone even had speaker function, so whoever it was would have to wait. If it was Camille returning my call I'd see her soon enough anyway, and if it was Adam checking in I'd ring him back when I got to the café.

I found parking a mere three blocks from the café and considered myself lucky. Heat or no heat, it was tourist season and Vieux Montréal was a Mecca for tourists, making available parking spaces as rare to spot as smiling faces on runway models.

My sundress hugged my body as I made my way along the cobblestone streets, keeping my eyes peeled for hoodie guy in case he popped out at me. He had yet to make an appearance and I was starting to doubt he would, but just in case I had the fake recipe journal in my bag. The bag was strung on papoose style and I clutched it to me like a parachute strapped to my front. And my feet already itched from heat collecting inside the sneakers I still wore in case I needed to make an impromptu sprint.

I made my way past kiosks of artists offering live portrait sketches, jewelry makers peddling their wares, and a string trio playing classical music that reminded me of something I'd heard at a wedding somewhere. Crowds gathered around the street performers and musicians, and I slowed for the narrow pathways, taking in bits of the shows as I went by. A clique of teenagers bumped me, and I got swept over to a semi-circle of onlookers formed around a young magician dressed in a top hat, shorts, and suspenders, no shirt, his face made up like a mime. He made a big show of searching for something in his nonexistent shirt pockets and the crowd laughed. I checked the time on my phone, wondering if I had time to watch the rest of the act before my meet-up with Camille. Eleven forty-five. Nope. Time to move along.

I slithered through the crowd and stopped for traffic at the last cross section before the café. A breeze wafted in from the port, helping ease the midday heat, and I let my lungs suck in a big gulp of cool air, my nose tickling with a musky brew mixed into the wind. I sniffed. I knew that musky scent. I scanned the line of people waiting to cross and spotted the man who had sat at my café table. The man Camille and Laurent called Grégoire.

A shiver ran up my spine and I dipped back, hoping he hadn't seen me, briefly lifting my sunglasses and peeking back at him again to be sure it was him. Yup. It was Grégoire all right. Same hair, different T-shirt and jeans. The jeans he'd worn the day before were dark and crisp, these were faded and had tears near the knees.

Traffic cleared and the crowd crested forward in a wave. I got caught in the sudden flow and I wrangled to stay behind Grégoire, watching to see if he was headed to the café again, too. When he reached the other side of the street, he took a sharp right into a wide alley lined with greenery and park benches. I glanced toward the café, torn. Probably I should run and get Camille, but I didn't want to lose sight of Grégoire. Maybe his meeting with his contact got moved to today. Maybe that's what he'd checked on his phone before he disappeared from our table. Maybe the contact wasn't a no-show but just couldn't make it. Scheduling conflict maybe or a heat meltdown. Maybe if I stayed on Grégoire's trail, this time the contact would show and I'd get to see who it was.

I pulled out my phone to call Camille and report the new turn of events, and I followed Grégoire into the alley.

13

---

*K*EEPING SOME DISTANCE, I strolled into the lane and discovered it wasn't an alley at all, but a narrow urban garden oasis fenced off at the end with a gateway leading to a vegetable patch. Several people were in the garden, some strolling, some flaked out on benches, some eating. Tourists maybe or locals on lunch break.

Grégoire stopped at a bench just past a couple eating picnic style beside a statue of a giant rabbit with a carrot fashioned into a fountain. Grégoire sat on the bench, and I pivoted sideways, keeping my face from view.

After a moment, he got up and ambled farther down the lane.

"He's on the move," I whispered into my phone to Camille. "Should I keep on him?" No response. "Camille?" Still nothing. I checked my phone to see if we were still connected. Ugh. Dead battery. In all the fuss of the night before I'd forgotten to recharge it. I had no way of knowing how much of our call had gone through before the phone died, but I hoped Camille heard most of it and was on her way.

Grégoire was rounding a bend into another wing of garden that banked off in an L from the veggie patch. I scurried after him, afraid I'd lose him. This time I found him sitting on another bench, this one under a large flowering tree with white sprigs so fresh their base was lime green. And he wasn't alone. A brunette woman sat with him. She was maybe mid-thirties wearing a mini floral skirt, a tank top, and a wide-brim sunhat, high-heeled sandals on her feet. And she had a box in her lap. A pink box with white polka dots and a big ribbon.

I dipped near a tree for coverage, its lowest branches still at least a foot above my head, leaving me feeling exposed. I scoped around for a better lookout. Nothing free close by, so I sank down to the base of the tree, pulled out the book in my bag, and held it up to my face. Just another urbanite taking a break in the secret garden park.

The sweet fragrance of the young white flowers from the tree across the path floated my way as I kept watch over the book top. Grégoire and the woman chatted amiably but quietly. Not like any spies I imagined, chocolate or otherwise. More like people who knew each other. Their words were too low for me to make out the language they spoke. I tried to read their lips but who was I kidding? I was no lip reader. What I needed was a bionic ear if I hoped to make out anything. Probably one with an instant translator feature built-in since the chances of them speaking English were slim. The woman's hat wasn't helping, either. It kept obscuring their faces with every dip of her head, making my view of their mouths intermittent at best.

I leaned forward when the woman passed the ribboned box to Grégoire. Sans ribbon, the box exactly matched the one Camille had at my house with the scrumptious chocolates inside. The likeness couldn't be a coincidence.

Grégoire slid the ribbon to the side, opened the box, bent to peer inside, and I heard a loud gasp. The couple turned to me and I froze, realizing with horror two things—that the gasp had come from me and that I was suddenly without camouflage. The sunflower journal was gone! Ripped from my hands leaving a stinging paper cut on one finger.

A flash of gray moved down the lane and I zeroed in on hoodie guy, journal clutched in his hand, dashing along the short L of the garden to what I figured was another exit on a neighboring street. From the opposite end of the lane, a flash of white came into view. Camille, strolling along the path wearing a pair of white skinny jeans, ankle boots, and a cream, silk sleeveless blouse. Her short blonde hair was damp and finger combed up and back. Her face was flawless fresh and pink cheeked with a dash of red lipstick and black-enhanced lashes. Designer sunglasses perched on her head, a car fob in one hand, and her mobile phone in the other.

Her eyes moved from me to the bench with Grégoire and the brunette then back my way, her stride leisure as she slowed to step across bits of grass to get to me.

"*Mais là*," she said. "Looks like I missed all the fun."

I winced at my paper cut and took a tissue from my bag to dab at the blood. "Hoodie guy just took off with the book," I told her. "And Grégoire is at one o'clock, over there on that bench with a woman."

"*Oui, je vois*. The plan is working perfectly this time. Your man with the hood will take the book back to his boss and with the tracker we'll learn who he is."

I stood and nudged Camille. "You think you should be talking about the plan with Grégoire and that woman right over there? She could be the contact."

Camille looked over at the couple and smiled. "That's Angélique, the *chocolatière*."

"You mean that's your client? And she's with Grégoire?"

Camille nodded. "Angélique and Grégoire are getting married."

I did a double take over to the bench. "Married? Yesterday you said the guy was stealing from her. Why on earth would she marry a guy who steals from her?"

"*C'est fou, no?* Angélique called early this morning and told us they were back together and everything was fine. That Grégoire was playing with her. He never meant to sell her recipes. Just get her attention. He didn't like that she put more time into her work than into him. They had a big blowout, broke up, and he threatened to ruin her. But it was only a threat. There never was a contact. He made it up."

"Seriously? You mean he didn't just work for her, he was her boyfriend? And that's how he gets her attention. By threatening theft? What happened to sending flowers? Or whisking her away for a weekend?"

Camille shrugged. "This is why I don't date. People who date go crazy."

I slid her a sideways glance. "What about that guy Luc you said you lived with?"

She waved her cell phone hand at me. "Luc is a lover not a boyfriend. Boyfriends and husbands are trouble."

She started back for the path and I joined her. She gave Angélique a passing nod as we went by but didn't stop. To maintain confidentiality maybe.

"What about hoodie guy?" I asked. "He's definitely real. He stole from me. Twice."

She nodded. "*Oui, oui.* My guess is when Grégoire was making a show of his threat he made some calls, word got out, and a real buyer got involved. Maybe even talked to Grégoire who brushed him off, so the buyer decided to make his own deal by stealing the recipes. We won't know for sure until we track the fake book."

"Right. But it won't hurt Angélique even if the buyer does get the recipes from hoodie guy because they're not her real ones."

"*Exactement.*"

We got to the street and ended up back at the kiosks.

"Then why bother even tracking the sunflower journal?" I said. "Your job is done. You kyboshed whatever spy business this was or wasn't and made the recipe trade you were supposed to, so really it's an 'alls well that ends well' thing isn't it?"

Camille pocketed her fob and fingered a necklace at a kiosk shielded by a giant white umbrella. "Laurent doesn't agree. For him all is not well just yet."

"You mean because he still wants to find the real buyer?"

She shook her head and moved on to a set of dangling earrings, held them next to her face, and peered into a mirror set onto the kiosk wall. Her eyes drifted to me in the reflection as she said, "Because you still don't have back your book."

14

I HAD ALL but given up on my book. Any hopes I had of getting it from hoodie guy were dashed when he made his mad dash and snatched the sunflower book from my hands. So I didn't know what to say to Camille's announcement. So I said nothing, forming my thoughts, as we wound our way through the kiosks, stopping to browse here and there, eventually finding ourselves standing by the café patio where we'd met.

"*Déjeuner?*" Camille said, hooking her thumb at the café door.

Hmm. *Déjeuner?* Wasn't that breakfast? "I had breakfast, but I could go for some lunch," I told her. Not to mention a break from the heat. Kiosk browsing on a hot day was much more sweat inducing than window shopping in a mall. "My treat."

She smiled and headed inside. "*Déjeuner* is lunch. *Petit déjeuner* is breakfast."

Ah. Good note.

When we got in line to order, her phone buzzed with incoming text. She checked it and moved us back out of line. "Lunch will have to wait. *C'est un texto d'*Angélique. Something's wrong."

She turned the phone for me to see the message. "SOS" in capital letters. Followed by *"Choco d'Ange."*

"I get the first bit but what's the second?" I asked.

"The name of the store of Angélique."

"Is the store close by?"

Camille shook her head. "In the Plateau. About twenty minutes by car."

Probably that was Camille speak for drive time. Probably it was more like thirty to forty minutes for the rest of us. Especially at midday.

I pointed off in the distance, unsure if I should offer to help or if that would be an intrusion. Or maybe make a rain check offer on the lunch. "Well, um, I'm parked that-a-way."

"Meter or lot?"

I was guessing she was asking where I'd parked. "Lot," I told her.

"Leave it," she said. "We'll take my car."

All righty, then help it is. I smiled, happy to get to help but also happy my curiosity wouldn't go unmet. I was dying to know what Angélique's SOS was about.

I followed Camille just over a block to a bank of cars parked near the port. Her car was wedged in near the middle, the passenger side of the car skimming the yellow parking line, the driver's side crowded in by a monster SUV.

"Attends ici," she said, pointing to the ground before she turned herself sideways, inched her way to the driver's door, edged the door open, and got in. When she backed out, she idled, and I got in, closing my door as she sped away.

Barely twenty minutes later, after what felt like a race through a maze that left my stomach back about twelve blocks earlier, Camille pulled her car over in front of a stone house with a bay window, a short iron fence, and a large, limited-hours parking sign stuck in the slender strip of dirt and grass between the fence and the sidewalk. Up and down the street were more houses. Not a store in sight. From what I could tell on my speedy ride over, commercial stretches in the area had little street parking so it was a good bet side streets were the main parking option. Probably not very popular with home owners wanting to keep the street clear for their own cars, hence the limited parking times.

We got out, and I gestured to the sign, thinking Camille could be cutting it close with the end allowable parking time. Not to mention the end of her car, which was covering half a slender laneway which I suspected belonged to the house.

Camille waved a dismissive arm at me, sweeping the arm across the road, and I craned my head to take in the other side of the street crammed with cars nose to bumper. None of those cars seemed to cover laneways, but I took her point. Probably we were lucky to nab even this spot.

"*Allons-y*," Camille said, heading up the road.

At the top of the street we crossed to the far side and walked nearly two blocks until we reached a slim storefront with a pink awning fringed with white polka dots. The glass storefront was etched with *Choco d'Ange* in large fancy lettering, elongated figures of angels eating chocolates framing the words. To the left, a white wooden-framed door with a stained glass insert was set in and up a step.

A bell tinkled when we went inside, and two heads poked up from behind a long display counter filled with truffles and *carrés*. Behind the counter, walls were painted sky blue with clouds skimming the ceiling. Short white shelves attached to the wall were filled with pink boxes, various cups, and decorative wrappers, with spools of cellophane and ribbons on rollers below the shelves. The tile floor in front of the display case was littered with broken chocolate bits, wrappers, ribbons, and sprinkles.

I stepped over a splotch of what looked like chocolate mousse filling, and a white cat leapt onto the counter in front of me, knocking over a stack of cute heart tins.

"*Arrête-le!*" Angélique called out, her full body coming into view as she skirted around the counter.

Behind her, Grégoire, the other head to pop up, scrambled after the cat. "*Menace*," he said.

Instinctively, I reached for the cat and cradled her to me. Her quickened heart pattered against my chest and her limbs went slack.

Angélique and Grégoire looked at each other. It was then I noticed the mini pet carrier in Angélique's hand.

Bursts of French words rocketed around the shop along with lots of finger pointing. The cat shivered against me, and I tried to cover her ears.

"*Ça suffit!*" Camille finally said. "*Enough!*" She turned to me. "Do you like cats?"

"Excuse me?" I said, my own ears still ringing from the verbal cacophony. "What was that about the cat?"

Camille drummed her fingers on the counter. "I said, do you like cats?"

"Cats? Sure. I like all pets." Well except maybe mice and rats. No New Yorker I knew was crazy about mice and rats, and tucking them up in cages didn't help their appeal for a lot of us. I had a live and let live attitude about them, happy they existed, just preferring their existence be out in a field somewhere running free.

"*Alors c'est réglé*," Camille said, turning her attention back to Angélique and Grégoire. "Lora can take the cat."

I looked down at the white fluff in my arms. "This cat? You're offering me this cat?"

"Yes, yes," Angélique said, dropping the carrier, running back around the counter, and emerging with a bag of kitty litter in one hand and cat kibble in the other. "She's very sweet. You will see. She's quiet and *tranquille*." She glanced at Camille. "*Tranguille* in English?"

"Calm," Camille said.

My eyes took in the mess of chocolate, tins, and sprinkles on the floor.

"The cat's been living in the back of the store," Camille explained. "But now that Angélique and Grégoire are getting married they're moving the store to Québec City." She threw a narrowed eyebrow look Grégoire's way. "Grégoire does not want to take the cat."

I stroked the cat with my fingertips. No wonder she was upset. Nobody likes to feel unwanted. Or live with the feeling indefinitely while some move was planned. "Of course I'll take her," I said. "What's her name?"

"*Minou*," Angélique told me.

Minou. Not exactly original but kinda cute.

A few minutes later we were back on the street. I had *Minou* in the carrier, and Camille had the food and the litter and a large pink box with white polka dots.

"*This* was the emergency?" I said as we trudged up the road. "How is a cat a PI emergency?"

"It's not. It's an Angélique emergency."

"Wow when I saw on your agency website that you offered a bunch of services, I didn't know they were so personal."

"*Mais voyons.* They're not. Not for regular clients. Angélique also happens to be family. A second cousin."

We got to Camille's car. I waited for her to bleep it open, but instead she turned into the iron gate leading to the stone house where we'd parked. A house I now saw had a simple black plaque bearing *Investigations C&C*, the name of Laurent and Camille's PI firm. That explained Camille's *laissez faire* attitude about parking half in the laneway.

"*Deux minutes,*" she said, setting the kitty litter and cat food down and unlocking the door. "I'll take you to your car in a sec."

She left the food and litter on the stoop and went in, waiting just inside for me before she shut the door. We went through a second door into a foyer kitted out with a table, two chairs, and some file cabinets. Camille set the pink box on the table and disappeared through another doorway to the back of the foyer. A powder room by the looks of it from the glimpse I got before she closed the door and I heard a tap run.

I placed *Minou's* carrier on a chair and looked around. Another door beside the powder room led to a kitchenette, and two more doors sat to the side, one closed, one open, giving me a view of a large armoire in the corner, a desk and chair in the center, and a window seat in the bay window overlooking the street. Walls throughout the place were painted a cream tone, the floors were light wood, and the doorframes ornate.

Camille came out of the washroom, her face refreshed, and after a quick ask if she minded me using the facilities, I went in. When I got out, Camille was in the front room with *Minou* in the window seat. Camille had the pink box open in her lap and was eating a chocolate and looking blissful. *Minou* was still in her carrier, looking miffed.

"*Tiens,*" Camille said, holding out the pink box.

I reached in to select a chocolate.

"*Non, non.* Take the whole thing. The box is for you. A thank you from Angélique for taking *Minou.*"

Wow. The box was big enough to hold shoes. And heavy, too, I realized after relieving Camille of the chocolates. That was a lot of thank you.

I looked over at the carrier. "Really I'm happy to help. I really do love cats. But I gotta say, I'm still a bit confused about Angélique and Grégoire. I don't get how she can be marrying him after what he did with all the stealing stuff and then now making her give up her cat."

Camille nodded. "Like I said, love is making her crazy. But the cat she found in the alley behind the store and let her stay. *Minou* was not so much her cat as her tenant. And *Minou* might not like Québec City. It can get colder than Montréal in the winter. *Minou* doesn't like the cold."

I smiled at *Minou*. Something we had in common already. She scratched at the mesh front of the carrier and I took that as my cue.

"Probably it's time I got this little girl to her new home," I said.

"So?" Camille said as we gathered up *Minou* and her gear, made our way out, and settled into the Jetta. "The café tomorrow for lunch?"

"You mean me and you?"

Camille laughed. "*Bien sûr*. Who else is here? We're friends, no? We have a sleepover, we break chocolate, we talk about *nos hommes*. And friends have lunch, right?"

I smiled and let my head slip onto the headrest. "Right."

15

"IT'S A CAT," Adam said.

On the way back to my car, I'd borrowed Camille's phone and checked in with Adam. Since the update call I'd promised him that morning was long overdue, I prepared myself for a long angry rant, but instead he was apologetic because his work crisis had kept him too busy to monitor his own phone. And then he was happy my part in the chocolate spy thing was over. Still, I didn't think it was a good idea to push my good fortune by telling him about *Minou* over the phone. *Minou* I saved for a surprise.

We both stood looking down at *Minou* who sat tenuously on the couch where I'd placed her after removing her from her carrier. She'd jumped up to the sofa back and been glaring down at Pong ever since she arrived. Pong, for her part, stared up at the cat, barking periodically and walking the perimeter of the couch like she was patrolling prison grounds.

Adam stretched his hand out for the cat to sniff. "I haven't had a cat since I was a kid. Is this one a boy or a girl?"

"Girl. Her name is *Minou.*"

Adam tried out the name and *Minou* ignored him. He went to the kitchen and came back with a new black shoelace he tore out of a package.

"Here, *Minou,*" he said, dragging the string across the couch cushions.

Minou shot Adam a "that is so lame" look and Adam stopped.

"Geez," Adam said. "My other cat loved string."

Pong, not to be left out of game time, dashed to get her ball in the corner, came back and mouth threw it at Adam's feet. *Minou* lunged off of the couch and tackled the ball, throwing her body down sideways, clutching the ball to her mid section, and scratching at the ball with all four feet. Pong sat on her haunches, head tilted, and whined.

Suddenly *Minou* released the ball and catapulted it under the coffee table clear through to the dining room where Pong fetched it, brought it back, and dropped it. *Minou* knocked the ball again, this time towards the rocking chair and Pong repeated her fetch routine.

Adam wrapped an arm around me and pulled me snug. "Looks like string's out and ball's in."

"So you're okay with having a new pet?"

"Who could say no to that face?" Adam said, watching as *Minou* and Pong tightened up their act so they were practically passing the ball back and forth along the floor until Pong got too close and *Minou* gave her nose a warning tap.

We both held our breath and released it when war didn't break out and the game started up anew.

"Good one, *Minou,*" Adam said when she made a particularly tricky pass and Pong knocked it back with her snout.

Minou ignored Adam again.

"Are you sure this cat's name is *Minou?*" Adam asked me. "She never responds to it."

Hmm. This was true. She never reacted to it when I'd spoken to her in the car ride home, either.

"Why don't we call her Ping? You know to go along with Pong like ping pong?" Adam said. "They make great ping pong partners in their game here."

I smiled. Watching them play *was* like watching a game of table tennis. And the cat was as white as a ping pong ball. "May as well," I said as we left the pets to their game and wandered into the kitchen to get dinner started.

"By the way, I'm sorry you didn't get your book back," Adam said coming up behind me. "I hate to say 'I told you so,' but—" he held up both hands and did a shoulder raise move, "I'm not surprised."

"I know," I said, moving to the sink to fill a pot of water to make pasta for a cold salad. "But I still can't believe it's gone."

Adam left the room briefly then came over to me as I set the pot on the stove. He waited until I turned around and he passed me a purple bag with bows dangling from the handles. "I know this doesn't make up for it, but I hope it helps."

Wow. A new cat, a new friend, a whack of chocolate, and now a gift! This day was turning out pretty good. I peeked inside the bag and pulled out a wad of tissue paper, unwrapped it, and found myself holding a copy of *Persuasion*.

"I know it's not a special early edition like the one your parents gave you, but it's an anniversary one."

"Wow. Thanks," I said, giving him a big kiss. "It's lovely." And it was. A beautifully bound edition with vintage-feel paper. The kind of gift only a really thoughtful boyfriend would give. Which made me kiss him again and add "thoughtful boyfriend" to my list of good things from the day.

. . .

THE HEAT WAVE broke by morning. More *Easy Bake Oven* level heat than red hot griddle. I got to the café early and grabbed a table outside, so I could spot Camille when she arrived. I people watched as I waited, admiring all the pretty summer outfits and listening in on snippets of passing conversations, pleased I even understood some of the French bits if I concentrated really hard.

I was so entrenched I almost didn't hear my phone ring, managing to free it from my purse just in time to answer. The caller was Camille, letting me know she'd be a few minutes late. I clicked off and noticed the voicemail icon showing an unheard message, and I remembered about the call I'd let through the day before while I was driving. When I plugged my phone in to recharge before bed, I'd forgotten all about the missed call. I contemplated deleting the message since it was likely from Camille or Adam and now unneeded, but curiosity had me punching in my code to listen.

A women's voice I didn't recognize came through. She identified herself and a spark ran through me. An interviewer from one of the jobs I'd applied to and hadn't been turned away from immediately after the meeting. As I listened to her message, my spark fizzled into an ember. She was calling with regrets I didn't get the job. She explained how well suited I'd been and how sorry she was she couldn't hire me, but that her hands were tied because of the language thing. Not a big surprise, but still I sighed when I pressed the delete button.

I tossed the phone in my bag, zippered it closed, and looked up as a shadow shaded my table. Beyond the shadow was a figure of a man, hair strands straying outward to the glow of sun backlighting his blue shirt and dark jeans like a shadow-box photograph. But this man was no stranger lurking to my side. I recognized this man straight away. Laurent, Camille's brother.

"This seat taken?" he said. The words were English but the French accent so strong it came off as a foreign phrase.

I smiled despite my disappointment about my latest lost job.

"Not yet," I said.

Laurent slid the empty chair across from me back and sat down, edging the chair closer to the table. He removed his sunglasses, making me glad I'd kept mine on to shield me from the intensity of his gaze. His eyes may have been dark but they were also penetrating. Probably a look he'd honed during his cop days to make suspects squirm during interrogations.

"I won't stay long," he said. "I know you're meeting Camille."

"Yup. Now that this spy business is over, we're having a lunch date." I crossed my arms, placing my elbows on the table, and leaned in, keeping my voice low. "And now that it's over, you can tell me. You didn't really buy into this corporate espionage thing, right? I mean spies don't really meet in restaurants and pass secrets, right?"

Laurent emulated my elbow move and bent his head close to mine. "*Non et oui*," he whispered.

"What does that mean exactly?"

He grinned. "It means I was a cop. I've seen a lot and heard about even more. And nothing surprises me."

"Nothing?"

He straightened his head to meet my eyes. "*Bon ben*. Almost nothing."

He reached behind him on the chair, pulled something from the back of the seat, and slipped the something across the table to me. A package wrapped in tissue paper closed with twine.

"What's this?"

"Open it and find out," he said.

I undid the twine bow and let the tissue fall open, a splash of blue coming into view. A rush of heat fluttered below my skin. "Is this what I think it is?" I said, gingerly spreading the tissue paper wider. "My book! You found it!" I jumped up, ran around the table and hugged him, clasping the book to my chest. "Thank you! Thank you! I can't believe you actually found it."

I spun back to my chair, flipped the book open to where my mom had written her inscription to see it was still there. I let the pages sift through my fingers, amazed to find the book in almost the same condition as before it had gone astray. Just a few smudge marks on the outside. Sweaty finger blots probably. And a folded sheet of paper tucked inside the back cover. I unfolded it to find the list of references I'd taken with me to the interview, likely stuck in the book when I'd jammed the paper into my purse after my meeting. My contact info made up the header of the page, probably how hoodie guy had found out where I lived.

"I can't tell you how much this means to me!" I said, closing the book up tight. "How much do I owe you?"

Laurent's brows furrowed. "Owe me?"

"For tracking down my book. I can't imagine what you went through to get it back. I have to pay you something for your trouble."

Laurent shrugged. Like it was no trouble at all to track the book to wherever hoodie guy had taken it. Like whatever he'd had to do to repossess the book had been nothing. Which I knew very well wasn't true, but this shrugging thing seemed to be a Caron family trait.

"Consider it a welcome gift," he said and stood, tucking the chair into its slot at the table.

"A gift?"

He nodded. "Besides, you did us a favor by helping with

Angélique. You did a good job passing along the fake book. In another life, maybe you *were* a spy."

"I have to admit it was kinda fun. Maybe I should consider a career change."

Laurent smiled as he slid on his sunglasses. "Maybe."

⚜

ACKNOWLEDGMENTS

Big thanks to my family, friends, and early readers. And to all the professionals who have shared their expertise with me. Much appreciated. All liberties I take stretching that expertise are entirely mine;)

And huge thanks to my French editor, Maud L. for her wise input and for keeping all that is the *belle province* of Québec real.

Of course, this book may never have come about if not for readers wanting to know more about Lora and the Carons early days together. So many thanks to those readers.

And to the people of Montréal for their generous hearts and constant inspiration. *Grand merci* :)

ABOUT THE AUTHOR

Katy Leen is the author of the Lora Weaver mystery novels. She credits her mom for sparking her lifelong love of stories through her own avid love of books. When she's not writing, Katy can be found listening to bookish and wellness podcasts, playing word games, reading, or hanging out with her hubby and family—always with a pup at her side and a cup of cocoa nearby.

Join Katy's *Nouvelles* newsletter where she shares more meanderings and insider info about the books:)

Pop by katyleen.com to check out the Q&A and her blog or Follow Katy at:

ALSO BY KATY LEEN

Series in Order

The First Faux Pas

The Nearly Nixed Noël (holiday novella)

The Pas de Deux

The Lost Love Liaison (Valentine novella)

The Ménage à Trois

The Easter Egg Ennui (Easter novella)

The Petit-Four Score

More Books

The Demi-Tasse Début (prequel novella)

The Lora Weaver Bundle

The Lora Weaver Holiday Boxed Set

The Lora Weaver series is still growing! Pop over to my website for news about the latest books.

The series is available in print, ebook, and audiobook.

I hope you join me for more of Lora's adventures:)

Happy reading!